Fraser's Line

Monica Carly

authorHOUSE®

AuthorHouse™ UK Ltd.
500 Avebury Boulevard
Central Milton Keynes, MK9 2BE
www.authorhouse.co.uk
Phone: 08001974150

First published by AuthorHouse 5/4/2009

ISBN: 978-1-4389-6006-7 (sc)

Printed in the United States of America
Bloomington, Indiana

This book is printed on acid-free paper.

DEDICATION

To my children, Dave and Sue.

ACKNOWLEDGEMENTS

I acknowledge with thanks the support of AuthorHouse and in particular my advisor Kevin Anthony. I am also grateful to Judy Taylor for her encouragement and editorial help, and to those relatives who, sadly, provided me with first-hand experience of such issues as epilepsy, and the problems of the elderly who live alone.

'If a man cares not for his roots how then can he care for his branches.' Doyle M. Davis.

Prologue

He ran from alleyway to alleyway, ducking and weaving to escape the artillery fire. It was more than two weeks since the uprising had begun and somehow he had managed to stay alive. On the first day of the resistance two boys had succeeded in climbing on to the roof of the headquarters in Muranowski Square and raising both the red and white Polish flag and the blue and white flag of the Jewish fighting organisation. These flags had fluttered in the breeze for four days, an act of defiance which had brought a brief glimmer of hope to the suffering prisoners before the Germans were able to remove them. In a desperate attempt to resist deportation and certain death he and his fellow prisoners had tried to breach the ghetto walls but against such military might they had failed. Armed with only a few pistols and some homemade explosive devices the brave attempts of the insurgents were doomed to failure and thousands had already died.

Now he knew he had little hope. It was said that there was an escape route through the sewers and he had decided to make an attempt to reach them. Every renewed effort to run cost his weak, malnourished body unbearable pain.

Sheltering briefly in a doorway, he undid his breast pocket and took out, for the hundredth time, a photograph of a beautiful woman and two tiny children. He gazed at it once more, his heart aching with longing. Then he returned it to his pocket and gathered his strength to drive himself on once more, but this time his moving figure was seen. From his vantage point on a rooftop just outside the wall SS-Hauptsturmfuhrer Karl Baecker unleashed a shower of bullets which abruptly ended the fugitive's progress. His shattered body lying in the dust, Ahron Cukierman, unsung hero of the Warsaw Ghetto Uprising, could fight no more.

Chapter 1

Spluttering angrily in the frying pan, the charred sausages split open with sudden force, disgorging their pink contents before Fraser's bemused glare. Why on earth did they do that? Whenever Edie had put a plate of his favourite dish in front of him the sausages were succulent, cylindrical, golden brown delights - moist and tender inside, with a heavenly aroma that set his mouth watering. Crowning this feast would be a mountain of soft, fluffy, mashed potato, topped by a glistening knob of butter caught in the act of melting, little golden rivulets starting to run down, destined to join the surrounding pool of rich, onion gravy below.

How well two such different items blended, forming a perfect union! The nebulous, white cloud danced gaily in the air above, almost mocking the earthy objects below, and yet needing them as a solid foundation. A marriage made in heaven, you might say. But now one half of the dish was missing, and what remained lacked life. Fraser had little appetite for what he saw on his plate.

He pondered on the irony that for years he had successfully designed and sold kitchens – but put him to work in one, and he was useless. Because Edie had been a wonderful cook who revelled in the role it had seemed natural to leave everything to her. How he had enjoyed her offerings! Perhaps there had been one or two disasters at the beginning, but they had turned into humorous memories and become something of a long-standing joke between them. Shall we have the chicken cooked or almost raw today? Would you like your potatoes with salt or sugar? But that had only been when they were first married – the natural errors of a new and slightly nervous young bride. In no time she had become confident, and her culinary skills surpassed his hopes and expectations. Every evening he had come home happy in the certain knowledge that his hunger pangs would be satisfied in an appealing and exciting way.

But marriage to Edie had been about much more than her appetising dinners – she had transformed his life. From the first moment he saw her he had been captivated by her looks, her charm, and her lively, fascinating personality. What she had seen in him he had never fathomed, but he counted himself amazingly fortunate that he had found her, and persuaded her to marry him. It had been thirty-one bewildering, tantalising, wonderful, heart-stopping years that suddenly ended seven weeks ago when, without warning, she fell, and died. It was, he was told, an aneurism, something totally unsuspected, and in a matter of seconds she was gone.

Now he had to live with an aching void which never left him in peace. People tried to make comforting remarks. The passage of time, he was told, would prove a wonderful healer. No one could suggest how you coped with the present, before that future time arrived when apparently the pain would have subsided. Edie had been everything to him, and his marriage a gift for which he had never ceased to be grateful.

Fraser tipped the sausages out of the pan - three blackened, distorted shapes against a white plate, looking miserably incomplete without that light topping of creamy mash. He'd have to get a slice of bread as an accompaniment. Fumbling in the bag for a piece he could hear Edie saying, 'Men cannot multitask. They have never learned how to think about several jobs at once.' She was quite right – he should have got that ready while the frying was going on; the sausages were already cooling down.

The telephone rang. Fraser cursed and picked up the receiver. Before he could say anything an urgent female voice said 'Hello! Fred?'

'No,' replied Fraser, 'it's not, it's…'

'Well where is he?' demanded the unfamiliar voice.

'I've no idea,' replied Fraser, reasonably.

'This is most annoying,' said the woman. 'I need to speak to him.'

'Perhaps you could try ringing him.'

'I just did, but you answered!' The female voice was becoming irritated.

'That's the thing.' Fraser was still trying to be calm. 'I answered because you rang *me*.'

'Well who are you?' she demanded.

'Fraser Coleman.'

'Who? Why would I ring you? I don't know you!'

'Look,' said Fraser, beginning to lose his cool, 'I answered because you rang me. I am Fraser Coleman, and you rang me. This is my house, and my telephone line, and you rang it. I don't know who you are, and I don't know anyone called Fred. And what's more, my sausages are going cold.

Not that I actually want to eat them,' he admitted honestly. 'They look burnt and they've split open.'

'There's no need to be rude,' replied the voice indignantly. 'All I asked you was why you answered instead of Fred. A civil answer never hurt anyone. And you had the heat up too high.' With that she banged the receiver down.

Slightly shaken by this unexpected exchange Fraser sat down and started work on his supper. After one mouthful, the telephone rang again. If it was another call from that mad woman he would find it difficult to restrain himself, but instead it was his elder daughter, Sarah.

'Hi Dad! Well, what's happening? Have you said anything to him?' Always so charming and deferential to her clients, Sarah seemed to consider it unnecessary to engage in any social niceties when addressing her father.

'Have I said what to who?'

'To whom.'

'What?'

'It's 'whom' after 'to'.'

'I'm grateful for the grammar lesson, but mystified about the point of this call. One extraordinary telephone conversation is enough for one day.'

'What extraordinary conversation?'

'Oh, never mind,' sighed Fraser. 'Let's just start at the beginning. What are you asking me?'

'You haven't forgotten I told you I was worried about the temperature in my fridge, have you? I spoke to you about it two days ago. I feel almost certain it's not running quite cold enough, and if that's so then the stuff in it must be going off, and I'm feeding my family suspect food! You said you'd ask John to come and test it, and you could get me a replacement if it was faulty.'

'I'm sorry,' said Fraser. 'I'm afraid it slipped my mind.'

'You promised, Dad, and nothing's been done about it! We might all die of food poisoning!'

Fraser had a sudden vision of Sarah, Michael and the twins all keeling over, clutching their stomachs – and it would, of course, be his fault. Sarah had a knack of making him feel responsible for any unfortunate events.

'All right, I'll come round myself first thing in the morning. Scout's honour.'

'Oh well, thanks. And by the way, are you managing all right?'

It was a bit of an afterthought, but at least she had asked.

'Since you mention it, I'm finding everyday life pretty difficult. Apart from missing your mother dreadfully, I can't cook. My sausages are revolting. They're all burnt on the outside and pink inside.'

Sarah softened. 'Look Dad, since it's Saturday tomorrow and we'll be at home, why don't you come for lunch? I've got a Shepherd's Pie in the freezer ready to cook, and I'm sure it'll stretch. I'll expect you at 1 o'clock. By the way, you had the heat turned up too high.'

By now the sausages were slowly congealing on the plate and Fraser pushed them aside. It was more than he could stomach. He might have to go and get fish and chips. Yes, perhaps that would be a good idea. On his way to the door he heard the telephone ring again.

'Fraser, dear!'

'Hello Mother! How nice to hear from you. I was going to ring you.'

'Were you, dear? Well, I just wanted to ask you how you were.'

'Oh, I'm all right, thanks. Look, I was going to come and see you tomorrow, but I have to go and see Sarah instead, so shall I come up on Sunday?'

'Thank you, dear, that would be nice. I don't suppose Edie will come, will she?

Fraser's heart gave a lurch. 'Well, no,' he said. Should he remind her? Poor Marjorie was getting so forgetful. 'Actually, Mother, perhaps you remember – Edie died a few weeks ago.' His voice trembled slightly as he said it.

'Oh my poor boy!' She was mortified. 'How could I forget that? I'm so sorry. Are you coping with things?'

'Yes, of course. Don't worry, Mother - I'm fine. And I'm looking forward to seeing you. Don't forget to line up any jobs you'd like me to do.'

'You are a good son. I don't know what I'd do without you. Sunday, you said? By the way, I don't know whether I asked you before, but are you still doing your kitchens? Isn't it time you retired? I worry about you – you seem to work so hard.'

His mother was not the first person to tell him he ought to consider retiring. Edie had been trying for some time to get him to cut down. She seemed to think he would do less if he reverted to a one-man band, as he had been at the beginning, before he joined forces with John. He had been with John for over 20 years now, and it worked so well he was loath to change the arrangement. Anyway, what would John think? It had made a good living for both of them, and on the whole was still doing so. What was the point of changing? He was touched by her argument that he should put in less effort, but he wasn't sure this would result from reverting to sole ownership. Now, of course, he wished he had taken her suggestion seriously – it was too late to try and please her on this matter.

He thought back to those early days. It was the time when fitted kitchens had suddenly become all the rage, and every wife up and down the country was putting pressure on her husband to have the new Formica worktops. Fraser had originally worked for a big kitchen company, but soon found their inefficiencies irksome. He'd visit a client, design the kitchen according to their preferences, and arrange a fitting. Then the client would be on the telephone, wanting to speak to him, because the company had let them down over the date, or some items were missing from the delivery, or something was damaged. He seemed to have the knack of soothing them down, and he always tried his best to make things right, often going far beyond the role of his design job. He had been known to drive over to the client with the missing cupboard, or set of drawer runners, in the evening, so that the job could be finished. The idea began to surface that if he ran the show himself he could make sure things went as well as was humanly possible. He liked things to run smoothly.

So Coleman's Kitchens was born. He found a supplier of good quality fitments in Germany, and at first he worked from home, ordering and fitting the units himself. By the time he married Edie he could afford to take on a small office, and he preferred not to have his work intruding on their private life.

One day he went to an exhibition of kitchen furniture, and by sheer chance fell into conversation with a man there who seemed to have had some similar experiences. Both had worked for national companies and had hated dealing with irate customers who had been disappointed by the service. Over a cup of coffee they had talked of this and the exorbitant prices these companies charged, and it appeared that doing a good job for clients at a reasonable price was as important to John Stanton as it was to Fraser. They exchanged details, and after some thought Fraser rang him. How would he feel about coming into a partnership? And so the arrangement came into being. Fraser dealt with the clients initially, and did the ordering. John undertook the installations. Fraser was delighted to find that John's standards matched his own. John was never happy unless he had done a perfect job. Sometimes at the beginning this did mean that the schedule was put out, as John would never rush a job, but when Fraser explained to the waiting client how much it mattered to them that everything was done to the client's total satisfaction the complaints usually died away. Fraser had a way of calming down anyone who was getting impatient and annoyed.

The partnership with John had been a success. Over the years they had become friends. Latterly Edie had started suggesting they did an outing as a foursome – such as go out for dinner, or perhaps visit a theatre. Fraser wasn't wild about this development since he had to spend time with Sadie, John's wife. Edie and John seemed to hit it off easily, and spent a lot of time laughing and chatting away together, but he found Sadie heavy going. She had little conversation and looked rather morose much of the time. Each time they came home he had been on the point of saying he didn't think these occasions were very successful, when Edie would forestall him by enthusing about what a good evening it had been, and what good company the Stantons were. As usual, he had bitten his tongue and let things continue.

John appeared to have been badly affected by Edie's death. He had called round to see Fraser, and the memory of that visit still left Fraser feeling uncomfortable – he did not like such a show of emotion. John had stood there awkwardly, looking moved – his eyes were moist – and he was wringing his hands.

'I'm so sorry, Fraser,' he had finally said. 'I don't know what else I can say – I'm so very, very sorry.'

'Thanks, John.' Fraser was fairly perfunctory, anxious to get rid of him.

'It doesn't make anything right, but I had to come and say it. I'm bitterly sorry.'

'So am I,' said Fraser.

'It should never have happened. Never. I can't imagine how you felt when you realised. I'd give anything for it not to have happened.'

Fraser was beginning to feel embarrassed. He couldn't understand why John was labouring the point, and he found it disturbing.

'I wish we could go back in time,' said John, 'and things could be as they were, when we were all happy.'

'Well, we can't. What's happened has happened. Now I must learn to come to terms with everything - there's no other option.'

'You must be so angry.' John hung his head.

'I'm devastated by it all, and I miss Edie every moment, but getting angry hardly helps, so if you don't mind, John, I think I'd like to be on my own now.'

'Yes, of course. I'm sorry. But look, Fraser, don't worry about the business. I'll put in all the hours it needs to keep things going for the time being – it's the least I can do.'

'I'm better working,' said Fraser. 'I need to have something to keep me busy – otherwise I'll just sit here and mope. But thanks, anyway.'

To his relief John had finally shuffled off, leaving Fraser to wonder why he had been hit so badly by Edie's death. He knew John had a very soft heart, and was touched that his own loss had had such a deep effect, but the emotion seemed excessive. After that conversation the two men didn't speak of personal things any more. They only communicated about work issues.

There was to be one more phone call before Fraser was able to go and buy his supper. It was his sister, Margaret. She had, it seemed, a very bright idea. Her friend Marion was giving a party the following Saturday, and she would be thrilled if Fraser would come. There wouldn't be very many people, and most of them Fraser would probably not be acquainted with, so he wouldn't have to put up with people not knowing what to say to him. Margaret was of the strong opinion that he really could not go on hiding away by himself. It seemed it was high time he tried to go out, and this would be the ideal occasion.

'No thanks.' Fraser was firm in his refusal. 'Please pass my thanks on to Marion, but I'm not in the mood for a party.'

Margaret tried all the arguments she could, but Fraser was adamant. Then she said, 'Mother's terribly worried about you. She keeps asking me if you are getting out anywhere. When I say no, you're just staying at home, she gets very upset.'

'She'd forgotten about it when she spoke to me a few moments ago. She asked me how Edie was!'

'I'm sure it was only a momentary aberration. She knows what's happened and how you've been suffering. Every time I speak to her she asks about you, and wants to know how you are coping. It would make her so happy to think that you were able to go out and join other people for a little while. She hates to think of you being so alone all the time.'

It was the only persuasive remark that could possibly have any effect on Fraser. He hesitated – Margaret seized her advantage, and before he knew it he had somehow agreed to go.

'Brilliant!' said Margaret. 'I'll tell Marion straight away.'

Damn, thought Fraser, as he went out for his fish and chips. Damn, damn, damn.

Chapter 2

'Lunch is ready! Everyone needs to sit up at the table now!' Announcements of mealtimes by Sarah required an immediate response. Woe betide the procrastinator who decided to finish the job in hand, or who, worse still, had failed to wash their hands prior to the pre-emptory invitation to the table. The interval between the time the family members were bidden to come and the final result of all chairs being occupied by diners in a state of complete readiness could be no more than thirty seconds or Sarah became flustered.

At one o'clock precisely the meal was served. The homemade Shepherd's Pie, brought to the table bubbling, with its golden crust browned to perfection, made a spectacular sight. How well Sarah looked after her family! Fraser was impressed by her competence and organisation.

'Magic!' breathed George, in eager anticipation.

Next the carrots and broccoli arrived – an attractive vegetable accompaniment with their contrasting colours, but this cut no ice with George.

'Yuk!' he shuddered. 'I really, really hate brolocci.'

'It's broccoli – and you have to eat it.' Kate adopted the

role of older sister, despite the fact that she had only beaten George into the world by twenty minutes.

'Greens do you good, old chap,' encouraged Michael. 'If you mix them up with that lovely potato you'll never even notice.'

'How do you mean, mix them up? Like a spell?'

'He's been bitten by the Harry Potter bug,' explained Sarah to Fraser.

'What bug? I haven't got a bug. Kate, have I got a bug?'

'Do be quiet and eat your dinner,' responded Kate, self-righteously.

'Thank you, Kate,' Sarah intervened. 'I think I can manage George. Now, I want both of you to show Grandpa how nicely and quietly you can eat up your dinner.'

Obediently the twins applied themselves to the job in hand. Fraser felt a sense of pride in his family, and began to be glad he had come. When he had arrived Sarah and Michael had been busy in the kitchen, working together in a unison that reflected the harmony between them. It reminded Fraser of how it had been between Edie and himself, slotting easily together. He was glad Sarah had made a happy marriage – fulfilled at home and at work, it seemed. At least that was one of his daughters settled. If only Joanna could find the right way forward.

He had tested the refrigerator, as Sarah had requested, and found it running perfectly correctly at minus four degrees. Although Sarah had seen his meter reading, she still wasn't fully convinced. However, Michael had taken over, and repeated what Fraser had said very firmly, so that in the end she had accepted it.

Fraser then made his way to the lounge to see what his grandchildren were doing, expecting his usual rapturous welcome, but Kate and George were unusually quiet. Typical six-year-olds, they could be boisterous and sometimes Fraser had a job keeping up with them. However, this time they had both appeared to be absorbed by their colouring books and did not look up.

Fraser had greeted them affectionately, and then sat down in the particular armchair which was always offered to him when he visited.

'What are you drawing, Georgie?' he had asked. Sarah disapproved of any variation on the name George, but as she wasn't in the room he had not worried. 'George' somehow seemed such a grown up name for a small child.

Kate had answered. It was strange how little girls assumed responsibility so early in life.

'Mummy said we were to stay out of the kitchen while she and Daddy are seeing to the lunch, so we're doing our activity books.'

'She said she'd better give you a good meal today,' George added. 'Grandpa, why did she want to give you a good meal? Are you very hungry?'

'I always enjoy your Mummy's meals,' Fraser replied. 'She's a very good cook.'

'Are you sad, Grandpa?' George asked.

'George!' Kate exploded. 'You know Mummy said you mustn't!'

'I didn't say it!' George retorted indignantly. 'I didn't! I only asked Grandpa if he was sad.'

Fraser was beginning to realise why the twins had been so subdued when he first arrived.

'What did Mummy tell you not to say?' he asked.

Kate had taken it on herself to explain. 'Mummy said we mustn't say anything about Grandma because it would make you sad.'

'I see. Well look, it's alright. Sometimes it helps to talk about the people you love when sad things have happened.'

'She's dead, isn't she?' George didn't believe in beating about bushes.

Fraser had wondered what concept of death a six-year-old could have. Should he talk about 'going to heaven'? Then there had come that distant memory of when he had been much the same age. What had his mother said? He could not remember.

'Grandma got ill,' he explained. 'Sometimes when people get old they get ill, and sometimes they are ill for a long time and they suffer a lot. Other people have a very short illness and they die, so it's good that they don't suffer.' He couldn't help thinking that it's those who are left behind who suffer - but that was a burden he had to carry – it was not something to put on these innocent young children.

'Are you ill?' George asked.

'Not at all,' Fraser assured him, 'so you have nothing to worry about. Of course we all miss Grandma a lot, and we shall always think of her, but you children mustn't be unhappy. She would not have wanted that.' He had changed the subject rapidly. 'Shall we get your train set out after lunch, George? Shall we see if Mummy says there'll be time?'

'Oh magic! Yes, please!' Then George's face had fallen. 'I think Mummy's going to make me sort my room out this afternoon.'

Fraser could not bear his disappointment. Sometimes Sarah was rather too hard on the children. Discipline was a good thing, of course, but he wondered if you could overdo it.

'I'll ask her,' he promised. 'Perhaps there'll be time.'

'Time for what?' Sarah had appeared with a jug of water.

'George and I would love to play with the train set after lunch. Kate might help us, too. That won't interfere with your plans, will it?'

'We'll see.' Sarah was obviously thinking fast. She had hoped Fraser would go fairly early as she had a lot of work to do over the weekend. On the other hand she was sorry for him, and she realised it could be therapeutic for him to have some time with the children and the train set, an activity all parties loved. And it would keep the children happily occupied for a while. 'I think we could fit that in for an hour after lunch,' she agreed, and George had been ecstatic.

The children continued to behave well during the meal. Once Kate had interrupted a conversation between Sarah and her father, but was quickly stopped. She had to wait until they had finished and was then given permission to speak. Fraser wondered if he and Edie had been so strict with the girls. It was difficult to remember, and he had to admit that he had left most of the disciplining to Edie.

Michael's mobile phone must have vibrated in his pocket, because he took it out and looked at it, and then put it away. A few minutes later he took it out again, and then asked to be excused for a moment. When he came back he seemed strained.

'I'm sorry, darling,' he said, 'but something rather urgent has come up, and I've really got to see to a delivery this afternoon. It will only take an hour – I'll be back in two hours at the outside. And I promise I'll do everything we had planned when I get back.'

'Oh no! Do you really have to go? We said we'd make it

a family day today, and Grandpa has come, and I do need you to be here.'

'I won't be long,' Michael promised. 'I'm sure the children will be happy playing trains with Grandpa, and I'll be back straight after, and I'll see they get their outside exercise, and then I'll do whatever other jobs you have lined up for me.'

Sarah was obviously fighting emotion, but she managed to put on something approaching a smile. 'Very well, but you're quite sure it won't be more than two hours?'

'Absolutely.' Michael was relieved. 'I'll help you clear away first, and I'll be back before you've noticed.'

When the meal was finished both the children chorused, 'Please may I get down?' and then George suddenly started racing round in small circles, imitating an aeroplane, and shouting: 'We're going to play trains! It's magic! We're going to play trains!' He banked steeply, spun round, crashed into a chair, and landed on the floor in a heap.

'George!' Sarah shouted. 'Stop that this minute! Any more of that rough behaviour and there'll be no trains for you!'

George stopped in his tracks and his face fell. He was obviously realising that a moment's thoughtless display of exuberance looked like jeopardising the very activity he had been anticipating so eagerly.

'Sorry, Mummy,' he said, anxiously. 'Sorry, sorry, Mummy. I won't do it again.' 'You certainly won't,' said Sarah firmly. 'If he's a naughty boy, Grandpa, you're to tell me straight away.'

'I'm quite sure he'll be as good as gold from now on,' said Fraser. 'Come on, children. Let's go and get the things out.'

The three of them absorbed themselves in setting up the track and watching the little trains chug under tunnels and through stations. To his amazement Fraser realised that for a short time he had forgotten the heavy ache in his heart. He was grateful for his grandchildren who had the gift, without any awareness of it, of bringing him comfort. He hoped perhaps he had brought them a little happiness too – for they did seem to have to function within the confines of a tight regime.

Sarah came to tell them it was time to start packing away. She thanked Fraser for keeping them so busy, as it had given her the chance to get some important jobs done.

'I've enjoyed it as much as they have,' he said. 'Perhaps more!'

As soon as Sarah had left the room Kate asked, 'Grandpa, is it alright for girls to play with trains?'

Fraser was taken aback. 'Of course! Why ever shouldn't it be?'

'Mummy says trains are a boys' thing,' said Kate, 'and I ought to like something more feminine.'

'I think anyone can enjoy playing with them when they're little.' Fraser tried to be tactful. 'Perhaps what Mummy means is that when you grow up you probably won't want to drive trains, which at the moment is what George thinks he wants to do. You might find something more interesting that appeals especially to girls. Anyway, trains are supposed to be children's things – and look at me, an old man, and I still love playing with them!'

'So it's alright now when I'm not grown up? I don't actually like dolls much.' The little girl looked so anxious Fraser felt sorry for her.

'Of course it is. And I hope I can watch you as you get a little older and see what things you like then.'

At that moment Michael arrived back home, smiling and in a very good mood. Fraser heard him greet his wife warmly, and then he came in to see them.

'Had a good time, children?'

'It was great!' said George. 'Really, really great! Will you come again soon, Grandpa?'

'Yes, I certainly will.' Fraser knew it was his cue to go now. The children both hugged him warmly, and he left for home feeling a little easier – until he remembered what he had agreed to do that evening.

Chapter 3

Gloomily Fraser rang the doorbell of Marion's house. Why on earth had he agreed to come to this party? He hated parties! He always had, and only went, as a young man, because Margaret managed somehow to bully him into it. It was different when he was married. Then, party going had become, if not actually enjoyable, quite acceptable. He had been proud to enter a room with Edie on his arm. He would watch the faces light up when she appeared, and he would smile smugly to himself, knowing what would happen.

He would inevitably end up in a quiet corner with a glass in his hand and watch the frenzied activity in the centre of the room. Edie would stand there looking poised, hand on hip, eyes glowing, a circle of men around her jostling for prime position. Her laugh would frequently break through the buzz of conversation, as she appeared to find each man who sought to interest her utterly fascinating – for a time, until another claimed her attention. She dazzled with her smile, her hand frequently resting gently on an arm, or shoulder. She would look round the little group and ask ingratiatingly for another drink, heaping praise on whoever supplied it.

Then suddenly she would move away, bored with the present company, and seek fresh excitement. The men would fall back, each feeling an acute loss of self esteem, as she moved off in another direction and began her entrancing routine all over again.

Occasionally she would come over to him and exclaim, 'Fraser, darling, do find my handbag - I can't think where I put it down!' Then she would lean towards him and whisper quietly, 'Shall we go home soon? I'm feeling rather tired.' He would get to his feet, all too happy to leave, but whether they actually left would depend on whether another man appeared at her elbow sparking fresh interest, in which case he might be still sitting there an hour or two later.

On these occasions Fraser knew that, although she might seem to be thrilled with all the men there, he would be the one to take her home, and this knowledge amply made up for any hours of tedium. Mostly she would be in a state of childlike excitement, eyes dancing, delighted to know that she had held centre stage, outshone her feminine rivals, lit sparks in most males there – who would no doubt try and contact her later, and who would get absolutely nowhere. She fed on the attention at the time and was satiated. It carried her through until another such opportunity came along.

When they arrived back she would still be in high spirits. She'd ask him if he had noticed what her female acquaintances had worn, and deride those who she considered lacked dress sense. She would laugh at some of the things the men had boasted about – which at the time had apparently so impressed her. And she would be so affectionate, that when they went to bed he was a very happy man. Yes, it would all be very worthwhile.

Just occasionally her mood would not be sustained once they had left the party and she would come home agitated and miserable. Fraser could only guess at the reason, but he would have an exhausting task on his hands trying to bring the colour back into her face and the light into her eyes. She would profess a headache, but he knew better. In some way she had, in her own eyes at least, failed to achieve the success she needed. He would try hard to boost her, telling her how wonderful she was, how no one had come anywhere near her, how everyone had told him how lovely she had looked, but somehow the mood would remain stubbornly unyielding. He would be helpless to do anything but wait for it to pass.

Fraser sighed. That was the past, and it was all over. Now he had to face arriving at a party on his own, and all of a sudden the tongue-tied man he had been in his twenties returned. He was about to turn tail and run, when the door opened. Marion — who had been a friend of Margaret's for many years - stood there overdoing the warm welcome.

'Fraser! How lovely to see you! I'm so glad you've come — we all are. We've all been thinking of you so much — how terrible it is for you. But you've done absolutely the right thing to come out — it's no good sitting on your own and moping — Edie would really not want you to do that!'

She was making it worse and worse. Emotions flooded through him — the overriding one being amazement at his own stupidity — fancy exposing himself to this! How soon could he leave?

He was about to mutter something about not being able to stay long when Margaret appeared and drew him in. 'Chin up,' she muttered. 'The first time is the worst. Look, I'll come and sit with you for a while.' She steered him into the room where people were mingling and those who knew him fell silent, not knowing what to say. Fraser smiled at them dumbly, and followed Margaret to a couple of chairs in the corner, where he sat and wished the proverbial ground would open and swallow him. This was even more difficult than he had anticipated, and he didn't know how he was going to get though it.

'Don't go away, Margaret,' he pleaded. 'I don't want anyone else telling me what a good thing I've done in coming out.'

'Don't be an ass,' said Margaret 'You've got to try and talk to people a bit. You're just wallowing in your misery, Fraser. Try and take an interest in someone else – it's a sure recipe for feeling a bit better.'

'I'm not interested in anyone else and I'm no good at pretending. I don't care if I don't speak to anyone all evening. I shan't be happy until I go home – and then I won't be anyway.'

Aware that he sounded like a spoiled child Fraser felt mildly ashamed, but still couldn't find the resources to lift his spirits. Margaret dutifully sat there and chatted about the family. First she mentioned Marjorie, and, as always, expressed her strong opinion that they must now consider putting her into a care home. Fraser found it difficult to contemplate this, realising how much she would hate it. Then Margaret asked him about Sarah and Joanna, and he responded monosyllabically. People came up in ones and twos and tried to offer condolences. Fraser felt awkward – he didn't know what to say. He must be putting a great big damper on this party, and that thought made him feel even worse.

Suddenly he realised Margaret had gone – the chair

next to him was empty, and he was alone. He was about to get up and make his escape when he saw Marion, the hostess, bearing down upon him with a rather well built woman trailing behind. He did not think he had seen this woman before – she was perhaps in her fifties, with a slightly swarthy complexion and long, dark hair.

'Fraser!' Marion's tone was hearty and Fraser cringed, guessing what was coming. 'I'm so glad I've found you! I don't think you'll have met Angela. She's a new acquaintance of mine, and hasn't long been living in the area.'

Fraser dutifully rose to his feet and held out his hand. They both sat down awkwardly, and neither spoke. Then Angela said: 'Isn't this absolutely awful!'

'Not much of a party,' agreed Fraser.

'Oh, I didn't mean the party. I meant the way friends have this terrible compulsion to bring together two people who are on their own. Just because we are now single is no guarantee we are going to have anything in common at all, but they can't leave us alone. Do you find the same thing?'

'I don't know,' said Fraser. 'This is the first time I've been out since I lost Edie, and I've been regretting it ever since I got here.'

'Why did you come in the first place?'

'My sister Margaret is Marion's friend, and she got me to come. I didn't want to at all, but my sister doesn't take no for an answer – I learned that pretty early in life.'

'Which one is she? Wait, don't tell me. I think I see a resemblance between you and that rather slim and handsomely featured woman in the black dress.'

'Are you always that flattering? I'd have said she had rather daunting looks and hasn't much awareness of how to dress.'

'Yes, but you're her brother, so you probably don't see her in quite the same light as other people do. My guess is she terrorised you when you were a small boy. Am I right?'

'She was certainly a very bossy sister, and she hasn't stopped yet.'

'Marion tells me you recently lost your wife. I'm so sorry.'

'Not half as sorry as I am,' said Fraser. Then, realising that sounded rather rude, he wondered how to retrieve the situation. 'Do you live near here?' he asked.

'In Twickenham, about half an hour's journey. Anyway, I've no desire to inflict small talk on you. I'll go and find someone else to bother for a little while, and as soon as I decently can I'll slip away.'

Suddenly he felt frightened of being abandoned, but on the other hand he didn't think he could bear staying much longer.

To his own surprise he heard himself saying, 'Look, I'm hating being here, and possibly you are too. I'd much rather be sitting away from any public gaze in a pub with a beer. I know a place up the road that's quite pleasant. Do you fancy a quick drink there?'

She hesitated for a moment, and then agreed that it sounded like a sensible idea.

'What's the pub called?'

'The Good Companions.'

She laughed. 'A touch optimistic, perhaps,' she replied, 'but I must admit playing truant would be just what the doctor ordered. We'd better not leave together – I'm sure you don't want to start up any rumours at this point, any more than I do. How shall we do this? Perhaps if you leave first, and wait outside in your car, I'll come out afterwards and follow you in mine.'

'I don't think I can handle the goodbye bit,' said Fraser. 'I know it sounds pathetic. I just want to disappear.'

Angela thought for a moment. 'I think I have it,' she said. 'I'll pretend I brought an umbrella, and can't find it. I'll create a bit of a commotion which will engage our hostess, and you can make your exit. How's that for a conspiracy?'

Fraser felt grateful to this kind stranger – she might look a little unusual, but she seemed to understand what he needed. What had she said about being on her own? He hadn't taken much notice, being too preoccupied with his own feelings. He felt he had been churlish, when she was being helpful. He made a mental note to ask her more about herself when they got to the pub.

Angela left, and then Fraser started to move in the direction of the door to the hall. He had almost made it when Margaret appeared and accosted him.

'Where are you going?' she asked. 'Not leaving yet, I hope.' 'Stop stalking me!' replied Fraser. 'I'm just looking for the little boys' room.'

'I can show you,' and she started to follow him.

'It's perfectly alright, Margaret,' he said rather huffily. 'I'm sure I'm old enough to find it on my own. You wait here and I'll be back shortly.'

The next minute he was in the hall – where he could hear voices raised – and then he was out of the front door!

Once they were settled in a reasonably quiet corner with their drinks Fraser asked, 'Have you been on your own for long?'

'Two years,' she replied. 'I won't insult you with platitudes about time healing. The fact is it goes on hurting, but I suppose I'm gradually learning to deal with it. It will better when I've been back to America where we were living and all the ends have been sewn up. I shall be going shortly, I think. What about you?'

'It's almost two months for me, and it hurts as if it was yesterday that she died – perhaps even more. It was so sudden, you see – there was no warning.'

'There was none for me either,' she replied. 'And I'll tell you something – I shall never get close to anyone again. Friends, yes – they help a lot in times of trouble – but a close relationship, no, never again.'

'So you don't subscribe to the 'It's better to have loved and lost than never...' sentiment?'

'Absolute trash!' she replied, surprisingly vehemently for someone who had seemed so gently spoken.

'I feel exactly the same,' he replied. 'There's no way I'm going to go through this again.'

'Tell me what you do with yourself. Are you still working? What do you do?'

'I'm in kitchens,' he said, simply. Instead of trying to prompt him further she looked at him with a smile, and waited. Fraser felt compelled to go on. He told her how his father had died when he was very young, and how he had always loved making things. 'I did a City and Guilds course in design. Then I joined a kitchen company. But it wasn't very satisfying working for someone else – I couldn't control things, and the complaints were mostly justified. I didn't like that. I wanted to run a business with the priorities I believed were important – I don't like fobbing customers off with promises that can't possibly be kept. So I managed to break away, and set up on my own. At first I worked from home, and did absolutely everything myself – finding the customers, ordering the supplies, and installing the kitchens. Gradually my business grew enough to take on a partner, but apart from John, and a girl to do the books, that's as far as I ever wanted it to go. Otherwise you start losing control again.' He'd got so involved in his account for a moment he'd almost forgotten that this woman opposite was a total stranger. Feeling he was going on too long, he began to apologise.

'Not at all – I'm interested in people and rather nosy about what their lives are all about,' she said. 'Do you have a family?'

He told her about Sarah and Joanna, and about Sarah's family.

'As a matter of fact I had my lunch there today, and spent a glorious afternoon playing trains with George and Kate. Do you know,' he said, leaning towards her a little, 'for the first time I actually forgot my own pain for an hour or so, I got so absorbed with what we were doing.'

'That's good,' she said, sounding as though it really was a source of pleasure to her that he had experienced that brief relief. 'Is there anything else that helps?'

'Yes - seeing my lovely 85-year-old mother. Tomorrow I shall be visiting her. And she always makes me feel comforted, even if she doesn't always remember that Edie has died.'

He started to tell her of his concerns about his mother, living on her own, and her increasing frailty and forgetfulness.

'The way your eyes are glowing when you talk about your mother,' she said, 'I can see you have a tremendous fondness for her. Did she bring you and your sister up entirely on her own?'

'She did, and a marvellous job she made of it. She has always been the best mother in the world – amazingly strong, and caring. I really want to do the right thing by her now. Margaret's pressing for her to go into a care home, but I know she would hate it. I go and see her as often as I can, and I'll try and visit more frequently. I think I may give work up soon, or at least make it part time. She deserves to be cared for now -she's done so much for us.'

'You have a lot of concerns,' she said.

'I suppose no more than other people. I imagine you have a fair number too.'

'Some,' she agreed. 'Look, I think I probably should get back now – I'm going to visit some friends myself tomorrow, and have a fair amount of driving to do.'

'I'm grateful to you for rescuing me from a black hole this evening,' he said. 'I had been dreading it, and it was turning out to be a very deep black hole – but thanks to you the evening hasn't been all bad.'

She smiled. 'Perhaps the pub was more aptly named than we realised. Anyway, I'm glad if I've been able to help you, as that helps me too. Perhaps I can be of some use in the future if you feel the need of an ear to bend. I wonder if, perhaps, you would like to have my phone number? Just in case you should feel you want to speak to someone?'

'Thank you, I should like that,' he said, aware that initially his behaviour had been unfriendly.

She fished in her handbag for a scrap of paper and wrote her name – Angela – and the number. Then she passed it over to him.

'You've actually been a bit of a godsend,' he said, taking the paper and stuffing it into his jacket pocket. 'The thing is, all I know is that you're Angela. What is your surname?'

'It's Gabriel,' she replied. 'And now I must fly.'

Chapter 4

Marjorie stood at the window of the front room in her little house where she so often stood when she was expecting a visitor. It would be lovely to see Fraser drive up tomorrow – he was always so kind to her, and never told her what to do, which was more than you could say of Margaret. Her second name was bossy boots. Marjorie knew both her children worried about her, and that Margaret really only wanted to help her. She wished she was not a nuisance to them. One of the worst things about being so old was feeling you had become a burden to your children.

She found it hard that her memory let her down these days. She felt so ashamed that she had not remembered about Edie's death. Poor Fraser, she did so hope he had not been too hurt by her blunder. She knew he would forgive her, as he always did, but even so she wished she had not said it.

Even when she was not expecting anyone Marjorie often stood at the window and watched the world go by. People knew her in the small village and would look to see if she was there, and wave. Those who knew her best would mouth the question 'All right?', and she would nod, and they would pass on by. It was a comforting feeling.

Suddenly she felt rather tired and went to sit down. It wasn't just the world outside that was passing by – her personal world was doing so too. She was well aware that Margaret, and Fraser up to a point, wanted her to go into a home where she could be looked after. When they talked to her about it she would smile obligingly and nod, but she had no intention of doing so. She had lived in this cottage ever since her marriage, and she was determined she would stay there until they had to carry her out – preferably dead.

She loved both her children dearly, but knew in her heart of hearts that her favourite was Fraser. He was a good, kind man, and still, in a way, very vulnerable. She remembered him as a little boy, always happy, and busy, putting things together, or trying to make something, and wanting to help his mother. He was contented with simple pleasures – some materials from which he could make something, and a stick of barley sugar. Apart from the sweetness of it, the simple twisting design seemed to provide a pleasure of its own. And when things went wrong with what he was trying to do, as they inevitably did at times, he did not get into a temper. He raised those solemn brown eyes to her, with a look of pain and bewilderment which tore at her heart strings, silently beseeching her to make everything all right again.

Perhaps the worst sorrow she had to cope with was when he was only five years old, and she knew Allen was not coming back from the war. Her own suffering was one thing, but seeing her little son hurt by the knowledge was far, far worse. How could she explain it to him? All those books so patronisingly ready to dish out practical advice to new mothers were completely silent on the subject of death.

'Why won't Daddy come back?' he had asked. 'Doesn't he like us any more?'

'He loves us dearly,' said Marjorie, 'but he's had to go and live in heaven. He didn't want to leave us, but he couldn't help it. Some bad people have stopped him coming back.'

'Can't we go to heaven and fetch him?' pleaded Fraser, his little, anxious, uncomprehending face sending a knife through her.

'We have to make Daddy very proud of us,' said Marjorie. 'You'll be the man of the house now, and you'll be able to help me look after baby Margaret.'

He had drawn a deep breath and puffed up his chest. 'I'll help you,' he had said. And he did, as much as a little boy could. He never mentioned his Daddy again.

One of his favourite playthings was his meccano set. He started out with a basic box, and gradually she had added some extra parts. Sometimes he followed the illustrations, but at other times he created something of his own. He would produce a car, or a tractor, and his pride of possession when he was eight was a beautiful crane.

Ben, a classmate, came to play one afternoon. He did not have the same creative skills and watched in amazement as Fraser demonstrated how the crane worked, lifting small items on its hook. Ben kept trying to attach items that were too heavy and in danger of bending the tiny hook, but Fraser wouldn't let him, explaining that the crane wasn't designed for anything like that. Then, when Fraser left the room for a few moments, Ben picked up the crane, threw it on the floor, and stamped on it. Fraser couldn't believe that his prized creation was now a tangled mass of bent metal. He brought it to Marjorie, saying sadly, 'It won't work now.' Marjorie saw the bewilderment in his eyes, and the pain.

She felt helpless to retrieve the situation. Fraser couldn't grasp that anyone should want to spoil something so perfect – it was a side of life he had not come across before, and he never could understand it. The desire some people seemed to have to destroy what was good and beautiful was always beyond his comprehension.

Now Marjorie thought about her son and worried about him. Not only was he having to cope with the sudden loss of his wife, but she had things she had to tell him before it was too late. He was going to find it all so painful that she did not know if she could face it, but she had put it off far too long. She had turned over in her mind the prospect of going to her grave with her secret – but who would be left to give him any comfort? Margaret would support him – she was a fiercely loyal person, and very good-hearted – but she lacked any obvious warmth or gentleness. Fortunately Derek, her husband, seemed quite happy with her whatever her shortcomings. At any rate, their marriage had survived over the years.

But Fraser was different. He seemed blind at times. It never even occurred to him to question why Edie had stopped coming on the visits. It was lovely to have him to herself, and as far as she was concerned it was a blessing. When he rang to say he was coming she had always asked: 'Will Edie come with you?' But she knew what the answer would be, even if she did not know which excuse Edie would have provided on that particular occasion.

'No,' he'd say. 'She's got some shopping she must do,' or, 'She's got a bit of a sore throat,' or even 'She's gone to stay with her sister this weekend.' Then she would have a lovely few hours with Fraser. He would do some jobs for her, changing light bulbs, weeding her tiny garden, or carrying any heavy items she wanted moved. Then they would have tea, and chat over all sorts of things, before he left, with his usual warm hug and cheerful wave. She longed to see him the next day – and yet, on this occasion, she dreaded it.

How much would he remember of those early days when they were a complete family? She had no idea, and in filling in the blanks she would be forced to stir up the sad memories, and bring him more pain.

The weariness was setting in. She lay back in her chair aware that sleep was coming. Sometimes sleep was a blessing, but sometimes a curse because it had a way of opening up the recesses of her mind and parading a kaleidoscope of memories before her.

Chapter 5

The gloom of a November fog greeted Marjorie as she left the hospital about half past five that evening. She had been working at Charing Cross Hospital since seven o'clock in the morning, and had had only the briefest break for lunch. She should have left two hours earlier, but they were short-staffed, and she had been asked to stay on. In those days nursing was a tightly disciplined profession, with all the nurses terrified of Matron. The wards were run with regimental precision, and cleanliness and efficiency were the order of the day. Being asked to stay on after your normal shift had finished may have sounded like a request, but it was a brave nurse who refused.

The dark, cold evening felt distinctly unwelcoming as she started to ride her bicycle back to the tiny room she rented. There would, she remembered, be very little to eat. She had meant to do some shopping on the way home, but now it was too late – the shops would be shutting. Then she thought of that lovely little corner shop on Slopes Street with the grandiose name of Allan's Alimentary Arcade. That was usually open a bit longer than the others. She could at least pick up something there.

There were still lights inside, and she pushed open the shop door, which 'tinged', alerting the man inside to the fact that he had a late customer. He came over with a smile. He was a young man, with dark, wavy hair, a slightly prominent nose, and the kindest eyes Marjorie thought she had ever seen. She began to apologise but he brushed it aside. He spoke with what she thought was an Eastern European accent.

'I can see from your uniform that you are a nurse, a profession I admire very much. Please take your time to choose what you want – there is no rush. Have you been working at the hospital?'

'Yes, she said, 'at Charing Cross, and I had to stay on. I thought there would be plenty of time to get my shopping done on the way home, but now it's rather late. Are you always open at this time?'

'I am open until 6 pm, six days a week.' He said. 'I, too, believe in hard work. Can I help you in any way?'

'I'll have some eggs,' she said. 'They will be quick to cook.' She thought about bacon – that would have been rather nice – but her nurse's pay did not run to any luxuries. He put the eggs in a brown paper bag and waited for any further items. She bought some butter, which he weighed on to a piece of greaseproof paper, and wrapped, and a small loaf of bread. That would have to do.

'This is with my compliments,' he said, selecting four rashers of the best bacon, 'and in gratitude for the work you do. Both my parents were nursed at Guy's hospital before they died and I shall always be glad that they had such good care.' She tried to protest, but he would not hear of it. 'There is one more thing – I am trying a new brand of jam, and I am asking my customers for their opinion. There, it is in your bag, and I would be so pleased if you would call in and say if you thought it was good – when you have time, of course. Now I will carry your shopping outside for you.' He held the shop door open for her, and placed the items in the basket on the front of her bicycle.

'Thank you, Mr Allan. Thank you very much,' she said.

'No, no, it is Allan. That is my first name.' He smiled disarmingly, and returned to his shop. She had thought at the time that it was a very English name for someone whose slight accent betrayed the fact that English was not his first language.

She began to wheel the bicycle across the pavement towards the road, but at that moment a small boy suddenly hurtled round the corner and cannoned straight into the side of it. The force of his body knocked her over, and the bicycle out of her hands so that it fell, skidding along the pavement, and scattering the shopping in different directions. The boy was momentarily entangled with the bicycle on the pavement, but he extricated himself with amazing speed, and ran off, so she had to presume he was not hurt. She rushed to retrieve the eggs, but knew before she picked up the bag that they were broken from the stream of yellow liquid that was beginning to trickle out. Miraculously the jam jar seemed to be intact – it must have been cushioned by the basket in its first impact with the pavement.

The next moment Allan appeared beside her. 'Oh dear, dear, good lady, are you hurt?' He seemed most concerned. 'I heard the crash, but I did not see what happened.' He helped her to her feet and began to pick up the bicycle. 'Perhaps you would like to sit down for a few minutes? I have a chair in the shop.'

Marjorie felt embarrassed, and tried to protest that she was perfectly alright, and not at all damaged. By this time he had spotted the mangled eggs, and set about scooping as much of the mess as he could back into the bag.

'Is the rest of the shopping in good order?'

It seemed it was. He asked her to wait there and took away the dripping bag. In a moment he was back with another containing six fresh eggs.

'Oh no,' she said, horrified. 'You mustn't. I can't accept them – it's not fair on you.'

'Please.' His eyes were pleading. 'I wish so much that you take them. Please do.'

'I don't know how to thank you.'

'That is not necessary, but I hope you will come and tell me about the jam.' Then he picked up her bicycle, and began to straighten the handles. 'I think that should be useable now,' he said. 'What was it that happened?'

'A small boy appeared from nowhere, and went slap bang into me. But he's run off, so he must be unhurt.'

'I hope I catch him one of these days! I shall teach him some manners. Just when you were tired and wanted to get home. I do hope you are not injured.'

He seemed so concerned that she set off in something of a daze, which she put down to the shock of having been sent flying. There were a few bruises, she discovered, but nothing serious.

To her surprise she found she was now looking forward to going back, and she tried to work out how many days she should leave it. How long did it decently take to test jam? She didn't feel she could rush back the next day. And how could she thank him for his kindness? Suddenly a flash of inspiration came – she would use two of the eggs to make him a cake! And she could put jam in the middle from the jar he had given her!

She managed to wait three days, and after an early shift at the hospital she had time to come home and bake the cake. Thank goodness it turned out as it should – in fact it looked rather good. She got herself ready to leave, wanting to look as nice as she could, and, by the time she had changed her mind several times as to what to wear, the cake was cool enough to have the jam added. She wrapped it carefully, put it in her bicycle basket, and set off.

Cycling as smoothly as she could in order not to jolt the cake, she was pleased that she had thought of the idea – until a chilling possibility suddenly hit her. Suppose he had a wife? She couldn't possibly give him the cake then. Whatever would his wife think?

By the time she arrived and was leaning her bicycle up against his shop, not only did he have a wife – but a baby, or two, had arrived on the scene also. Well, she had to go back and say thank you, and give her opinion on the jam. That was perfectly in order.

Leaving the cake in the bicycle basket she pushed open the shop door. He looked up from serving a customer and his face was flooded with a look that seemed to say: 'This is the moment I have been waiting for!' But of course she was imagining it – a married man would not be thinking such thoughts.

She stood and waited until the customer had left. He came towards her his face lit with a dazzling smile. 'How good to see you again. I am so sorry for what happened. Were you much hurt?'

'Oh no, only a few bruises – I think the bicycle came off worse than I did.'

'I had been hoping you would come back – so that I could know you were all right. Did the eggs make it safely home this time?'

'Yes, they did, and I came to say thank you for being so kind, and I did like the jam.'

'The jam? Oh yes, the jam. I'm glad you thought it was good. Look, I am quite a handy person – would you let me look at your bicycle at the weekend and see if I could repair it a little?'

'Oh no – I couldn't possibly – you might…' This was the moment to ask but she couldn't think how to put it. 'You might need to do other things with your time.'

'Nothing that cannot wait a little longer.'

She was no further forward. She found herself blurting out 'Has your wife tried the jam?'

He hesitated. 'I'm not sure – I'd like to think she has.'

She looked confused, and her smile disappeared. He stepped towards her.

'Forgive me,' he said, 'I should not have said that. I have no wife. I live alone. You would not be taking my time away from anyone else.'

'Oh,' she said, 'then I could have given you the cake!'

It was his turn to look puzzled.

'I made you a cake – I used some of the eggs and jam you had given me because I wanted to thank you – but I hadn't stopped to think you might be married, I only thought of that on the way over, so when I got here I couldn't give it to you.' It all came out in a rush, and she was feeling rather silly.

'You did that for me? That was a very kind thought. I shall come outside and look at your bicycle.'

He squatted down and examined it. 'It has collected some scratches and dents. I cannot make it perfect, but I think I could improve it. Would you let me try? I could come and fetch it on Sunday.'

'Are you sure? I don't like to take your time – you have so little if you are in the shop all day.'

'I have an even better idea,' he said. 'Would you do me the honour of coming to the cinema with me on Saturday evening? If you came here at six o'clock I could lock the bicycle in my shop – and then I would see you safely home afterwards. I would be so happy if you would do that.'

Her heart suddenly felt so light she was in danger of sounding too enthusiastic. 'I should love to, thank you.'

'I will see you on Saturday, then.'

'Yes, see you on Saturday.' She picked up her bicycle and turned to go.

'Please may I have my cake?'

Was he laughing at her? The look was so kind and gentle she didn't mind if he was. Holding the cake he stood and watched her go until she was out of sight.

That Saturday evening at the cinema had been the start of it. She had felt completely happy in his company. He was entirely respectful and courteous, yet warm and friendly at the same time. They laughed over the film together, and then he escorted her home, first on the bus, and then walking. He made no attempt to touch her, but somehow she knew how he felt. When they parted he smiled that devastating smile, and said how happy she had made him, and he would do his best to repair the damage.

The next evening he was outside her house with her bicycle, restored, if not to its former glory, at least looking as if it had received some thoughtful attention. She felt quite safe in asking him into her tiny room for a cup of coffee, and found him easy to talk to, and cheerful company.

They began to spend as much of their spare time as they possibly could together. She made every attempt to secure Sunday as her day off, and then they would go out for the day. Sometimes they went for a cycle ride – he rode the delivery bike that he kept for young Reg to do the shop's errands – and perhaps took a picnic. She loved these days. There was a great deal of laughing, especially when they got lost, or caught in a heavy downfall of rain.

Sometimes she went to his house. The first time she saw it – a small cottage in a road of mediocre houses – she was impressed by the neat outer appearance. He apologised before they went in for his 'bachelor ways', but it was clean and tidy, if rather sparsely furnished. However, in the living room there was a piano. Somewhat to her surprise she found he was an accomplished pianist, and she spent many happy hours sitting next to him while he played beautiful lilting melodies that touched her heart. She loved to watch his hands moving capably over the keys and she knew he was beginning to mean a great deal to her.

And they talked. There was so much to learn about the other. He wanted to know what had happened before she came to the hospital, so she told him about her family home in St Albans. Her father was a solicitor in a flourishing law practice and made a comfortable living. She was an only child and he wanted her, if possible, to train for a career in law. Even if that did not prove possible, he certainly wanted her in an office-based environment. But Marjorie had had other ideas. Even when she was quite young she knew that she was attracted to nursing, and when the time came she was adamant that no other profession would do. It did not matter how much her parents warned her about the long hours and hard work, not to mention the poor rate of pay – nothing discouraged her. In the end they were forced to give in.

From the first day that she had embarked on her

training she knew this was what she wanted to do with her life. The more competent she became the more she revelled in what she could do to ease the suffering of sick people. It was so rewarding to see them smile when she approached, and when their health improved she took a real pride in their progress. She was devastated when a patient died.

Sometimes when she was working a late shift Allen would come to the hospital to meet her. It was wonderful to walk out and find him standing there quietly, watching for her. He would bring the bicycle, so they could cycle home together. One evening she came out looking very distressed. A little boy she had been nursing for some time had lost his fight with cancer.

'He was only six!' she had sobbed. 'His poor parents! How does anyone cope with a loss like that?'

He had put his arms round her and said, gently, 'Life can be very cruel.' She had found his presence marvellously comforting.

For his part, he told her how he and his parents had come to settle in England. Born and bred in Poland he became aware, at the beginning of the 1930s, that his parents were finding that life was becoming tough. They had owned a small grocery shop, but as the depression deepened, and the boycotts began, there seemed to be little future. He had an older sister, but she was much older than he was and had married. She did not want to leave, but his parents, already getting frail with the worry of it all, felt there were no prospects for their son and looked for a way of leaving. They had a cousin who had moved to England some time previously with whom they were able to make contact. He helped them with the arrangements, and in 1931, when Allen was sixteen, they came to Chiswick and just had enough money to set up their grocery shop. But the strain had been great, and three years ago his parents had died, within a few months of each other. Allen, who had worked in the shop by day, and attended Evening classes after work to learn English, took over the running of the shop. He changed its name from 'Coleman's Groceries' and gradually built it up, making a modest living, and continuing to live in the house his parents had bought.

'You must have been very lonely after they died,' Marjorie had commented.

'Yes, indeed I was, but I also counted myself lucky to have my life in England, and my small business. I believed that one day life would take a better turn for me and fulfil that other part of my life, but meanwhile I must work hard and make a success of the chance I had been given.'

On one of their picnics, they were finishing their sandwiches, sitting in a grassy field when it occurred to her to say, 'I knew from your accent that you weren't English, although you speak it very well. But your name sounds English. Was that your original name?'

'No,' he said. 'When we became British citizens we thought it best to change our names to something that fitted in better with our new environment.'

'What was it before?'

But before she got her answer he suddenly leapt to his feet and started slapping at various parts of himself, jumping about and batting at something in the air, and shouting, 'Go away! Shoo!'

Laughing, she got to her feet and tried to help him, although she couldn't spot where the offending insect was.

'Oh, it's gone now. I'm so sorry. Come, let's go before we are attacked again.'

In all the commotion she had forgotten about her

question, and had to wait some considerable time before she eventually learned the answer.

They continued to meet frequently, and to enjoy any spare time they had together. On one occasion they took the train up to London. First they stood outside Buckingham Palace and watched the Changing of the Guards. As they moved away he playfully adopted the solemn marching movements, until she was giggling helplessly. Then they went to St Paul's and climbed the 163 steps up to the Whispering Gallery. There they stood at opposite sides, turned to face the wall, and whispered each other's name – and the sound came floating round. Finally they went on a boat on the Thames. He held her hand as the outside world slowly drifted by and the feeling of tenderness and protection she had whenever she was with him was so overwhelming it was like living in a dream.

One Sunday that stayed very firmly in her memory was when they went to Brighton. They took the train early that morning and spent the whole day there. First they wandered about The Lanes. Then they spent a happy hour or two on the pier. After that they clambered over the pebbles down to the water's edge and stood, like children, sending spinning stones into the sea, trying to make them bounce. A mischievous wave broke higher on the beach than its predecessors and started swirling about their feet. Laughing they tried to avoid soaking shoes, jumping back up the beach, but Marjorie somehow lost her balance, tottered and fell. Allan tried to grab her but was too late.

'You're not hurt, are you?' Immediately his smile was replaced by a look of concern. He held her hands, drawing her up on to her feet, and the depth of feeling she saw in his eyes turned her knees to such jelly she was in danger of falling down again.

'I'm quite alright – really I am.' She began brushing her clothes free of the damp pebbles and sand.

'I don't ever want you to be hurt,' he said, suddenly very serious in his manner. 'I want to look after you so that you do not get hurt. I want to be your husband so that I can always care for you. Marjorie, please, would you be my wife?'

The proposal took her completely by surprise, but she answered without hesitating for an instant.

'Yes, I would like that.' She didn't feel she had said quite enough, so she added: 'Thank you.'

'Oh, it is for me to thank you! And I shall thank you every day of my life!' He snatched off his cap and hurled it high in the air. As it soared upwards he shouted out triumphantly, 'She said yes!' and spun round in a circle.

By then the cap had started its descent, but the wind had changed its path so that he had to lunge forward to catch it. In doing so he slipped and now it was his turn to find himself lying on the pebbles. They began laughing and he sat up looking rueful.

'It is true, what they say, that pride comes before a fall – for I am the proudest and happiest man on the whole earth!'

As they left the beach, with their arms wound round each other's waist, Marjorie thought she had never known that such intense joy existed.

They had a quiet wedding – just her parents, and a few other relatives, and guests - his neighbours, an elderly and very sweet couple, and the greengrocer who had a shop next door to his.

Initially her parents had been shocked when she had

announced that she was going to marry a man she had met in a shop three months previously. But by now they realised that when she had set her mind to something there was little point in trying to dissuade her. In any case, when she took him to meet them they saw for themselves how much the young people meant to each other, and they liked what they saw in him.

He decided to close the shop for a week, so that they could have a honeymoon. They took the train down to Torquay, where he had booked a small hotel. As the train puffed its way round the South Devon coast, in and out of the tunnels, and through the little towns of Dawlish and Teignmouth, they drank in the sight of the sea through the train window and were as excited as children going on holiday.

That week was a little bit of paradise for both of them. The first night they lay in each other's arms, not wanting to lose physical contact for a moment, and Marjorie was amazed at the depths of feeling his tenderness awakened in her.

At one point she whispered, 'Why me? And when did you know?'

'I knew from the first moment you came into my shop,' he answered. 'You stood there looking a little worried, your golden hair standing out against your dark nurse's cape – you were so beautiful - and I saw such spirit in you, and yet a vulnerability as well. I wanted to take you in my arms then and promise to look after you.'

'You might never have seen me again.'

'I had to make sure I did. So I'm afraid I resorted to a little trick, and now I feel so bad, because I want only to be completely honest with you.'

'A trick? Oh, I know – the jam! So that wasn't true at

all, about trying it out?'

'No, I'm so sorry. I couldn't think of anything else at the time. Please say you forgive me. I was desperate to have you come back.'

'Of course I do, silly. It worked, as you know. Anyway, I had to take a firm grip on myself or I would have run back to your shop the very next day! I think if you hadn't done your jam trick I would have thought up some reason to come, like making the cake.'

'Ah yes,' he said, 'the cake. I had to marry you after that – it was so delicious. But please tell me when you knew, and, if I may ask, why did you want to come back?'

'I knew that very first day,' she said. 'It was like a bolt from the blue. I was bowled over.'

'I think, my dearest one, that was not me. That was the small boy.'

'You were so kind – and you had such lovely eyes, and attractive smile – I thought I had never met anyone who was so handsome.'

'Now I am blushing,' he said. And they laughed and held each other closer.

When it was time to go back she went to live in his house, having given up her little rented room. He said she was welcome to do whatever she would like to make it more homely, and she happily set about adding some feminine touches, such as curtains and rugs, and some pictures and ornaments. To begin with she tried to continue nursing, but she found her heart was not in it in quite the same way, and in any case, within four months she knew she was pregnant.

When Fraser was born Allan was so overjoyed he could not stop beaming. He had been concerned throughout her pregnancy, and especially when she went into labour, and had given her all the support he could. In those days fathers were not at all welcomed during the birth, but the minute he was allowed to he rushed to her side and held her, tears of relief and joy on his face. Then he turned to look at his son.

'He's wonderful!' he said. 'May I pick him up?' He cradled the tiny baby and could not speak for a moment – his happiness and pride were boundless.

'What shall we call him?' he asked.

'Please, Allan, may we call him Fraser? I have always loved the name. And his second name must be Allan.'

'It shall be just as you like,' he said. 'Fraser is a very distinguished name. I am sure with that name my son will grow up to be a brilliant surgeon.'

'Oh, I thought it was a rather cosy and comfortable name,' she said, 'rather like an old slipper.'

'Now I am confused – I do not know whether he is to become a surgeon or a slipper!'

'Perhaps we don't need to worry – he will probably choose for himself. But, whatever it is, with a father like you he is bound to become a very fine man.'

'And he will be so proud when he finds out what a beautiful and wonderful mother he has.'

He had been a good father. He shared in all that had to be done far more than was usual. He would change nappies, and bath the baby, and when the pains of teething transformed the once placid baby into a bundle of screaming rage he would pace round the room with him on his shoulder, talking soothingly and sometimes singing little songs – some in Polish, which he dimly remembered.

Eighteen months later Margaret was born.

'Now,' he said, 'we are a complete family. What a clever wife I have – and so beautiful, even though she has had to go through all this twice.'

She thought she had no right to be so happy – to be loved, and cherished all the time was almost too good to be true. It seemed nothing could mar this bliss.

But the jackboots had begun to march across Europe. First Austria fell, then Czechoslovakia. It was clear Poland would be next.

'My people are enduring the most terrible sufferings,' he said. He did not need to say any more. She knew what he was thinking.

For two days he neither ate nor slept. He paced round the house and garden, and she knew his torment. She also knew what he would decide.

At last he came to her.

'I have to go,' he said. 'I cannot ignore my countrymen when they are enduring such terrible things.'

'But what can you possibly do?' she cried. 'You are not strong enough to do anything on your own. You will only get killed!'

'I have to go,' he said. 'I am so very sorry.'

In order not to prolong the agony he made his arrangements speedily. On the last night they lay clinging together as though both their hearts would break. There were tears, but then they tried to be strong for each other.

She stood at the door to watch him walk away down the street – a solitary man, carrying a small, light suitcase but weighed down by an unbearably heavy heart. She watched until he had gone out of sight, and even then she did not move for a long time. Finally, she turned and went back into the house.

She never saw him again.

Chapter 6

Fraser arrived about 11 o'clock on Sunday morning and greeted his mother warmly. She looked very frail, and it tore at his heart strings, but her smile was as warm and lovely as ever.

'Hello mother, darling! How are you?

'Well, thank you, Fraser dear. I'm well.'

'What about those swollen ankles? Has the doctor been able to suggest anything?'

'Oh, I'd forgotten about them. They really don't trouble me.'

Fraser was about to say something but Marjorie cut in to stop him. 'Now don't fuss, please Fraser. There's nothing wrong except that I seem to be getting more muddle-headed than ever. Do you know what I did yesterday?'

'Tell me,' said Fraser, settling into the armchair opposite her, and immediately making the room look cosy.

'You'll think me very silly. Well, I thought of two things I needed from the shops, and as it was such a nice, bright day I thought I could manage to go round to the corner shop. I do so love the little corner shop, even if it is difficult to find what you want. So much better than those huge supermarkets. Anyway, Celia, my neighbour, does my shopping there for me once a week. Isn't it kind of her? She's so good to me.'

Fraser nodded. He'd heard this refrain many times before.

'There were just two things I wanted, and I knew perfectly well what they were when I set off.'

'Did you write them down – the way we discussed before – to help you remember?'

'Of course I did, dear. I always try and do what you tell me. But when I got to the shop I couldn't find the piece of paper. I must have left it behind. Well I knew what the first thing was – that was butter – but I could not think of the other thing, no matter how hard I tried. So I wandered about the shop, pretending I was looking at the displays, and then suddenly I found myself in front of a tin of treacle – and so I knew!'

'You wanted some treacle?'

'No, of course not, dear. Whatever would I want treacle for?'

'I thought you said...' Fraser wasn't sure he was following.

'It was the T – that was what I wanted, Tea!'

'Oh!' cried Fraser. 'How clever of you! I don't think you've been a silly muddle-headed lady at all!'

'Well, yes I was, because you see, when I got home, I found I hadn't got the butter. So I bought the thing I'd forgotten, but I must have forgotten what I'd remembered.'

'Yes, I see, I think. Never mind, mother, I'll slip out and get you some now. It won't take long.'

'Get me some what?'

'The butter you came home without yesterday.'

'Oh no, you needn't trouble yourself doing that. I've got plenty of that.'

Fraser gave up. Before he could say anything Marjorie spoke again. 'Dear Fraser,' she said. 'It always makes me so happy to see you. You are such a good, kind son. No mother could ask for a better.'

'I wish I could do more, Mother. It does worry me that I am not on the doorstep.'

'You mustn't worry so. I know how to contact you if I need to, and you have your own life to lead.' She almost asked about Edie, but some flash of memory saved her. 'How are your two lovely daughters?' she enquired.

'Fine, I think. I had lunch with Sarah and Michael, and the twins yesterday. George, Kate and I spent a happy afternoon playing with the train set. I haven't actually heard from Joanna for a few days – I think she may be finding the loss of her mother very hard, since she's on her own, and she's rather younger and a lot less mature than Sarah. I wish she was more settled in life. She seems so restless, and doesn't really know which direction to go in. But look, I don't want you to trouble your head about that.'

'And what about you, dear? How are you?' Marjorie looked at him anxiously.

'Oh I'm managing all right, although of course I do find it difficult without Edie. Still, I went to a party yesterday evening, at Marion's.'

'Did you really? Oh I am so glad. That's made me feel really happy.'

'Margaret said it would please you.' He did not add that it was the only argument that had carried any weight when he was deciding whether he could manage to go. 'I can't pretend I'd have gone without Margaret's gentle persuasion.

55

Nor can I pretend I enjoyed it enormously. However, it was made rather better by a strange woman who appeared from nowhere, and unlike everyone else, seemed to know what to say. Now, Mother, you said there was a reason why you would like me to come today.'

'Yes, in fact I have two things I want to talk to you about. One's good, and the other isn't so nice.'

'Then let's start with the good news,' suggested Fraser.

'I think you'll be very pleased, because I had a problem that I didn't know I had, and now it's been all sorted out.'

'So tell me,' encouraged Fraser.

'It was so fortunate because the man happened to be passing, and he must have stopped outside. And when he did he must have looked up, and he saw that some of my roof tiles were missing. And what was even luckier, he happened to have some on his lorry. So he knocked at the door and told me, and apparently if I didn't do something about it the rain would leak through, what with winter not far away. He said he just had time to fit in the repair before his next appointment.'

Fraser groaned inwardly while trying to keep a pleased expression on his face. He couldn't bear to disappoint his mother.

'So I told him to go ahead, and it took him quite a long time. One thing was that he had to go and fetch some more tiles, because there were more needing to be replaced than he first thought. He must have had to go quite a distance, because he was a long time coming back. But he did get it finished, just in time to take me to the bank to get his payment. Wasn't that kind of him!'

Fraser struggled to control his voice. 'It's good that it's all finished. How much did you pay him?'

He said as I was such nice old lady he'd only charge me half price, so it was £2000. I thought it must have been a bit of a bargain. Just fancy, if we hadn't found out about the missing tiles I might have had water coming in before long. I knew you'd be pleased, so I've been longing to tell you.'

'I'll just have a look and make sure he's left it all absolutely in order,' Fraser said. He went outside and stood back far enough to see the roof. Without getting up a ladder it wasn't easy to tell, but he was fairly sure that the tiles were all in a very good state, and that there were just two fresh ones up there. He was angry, not only with the sort of con man who could prey on elderly ladies, but also with the bank. They must have been aware that this was the subject of much publicity. It had featured on 'Watchdog' and Fraser felt sure banks had been warned to be on the alert if an elderly client came in to draw out a large sum of money, accompanied by a rough trader, standing as discreetly in the background as possible. The damage was now done, and the important thing was not to upset his mother. At the same time he must try to get through to her that she should really leave everything to him. He knew she hated to be a nuisance, but he did not view it that way at all.

When he went back inside Marjorie seemed to have nodded off in her chair. The sound of his entry roused her. 'What did you think?' she asked anxiously.

'I can see the new tiles he's put there, and everything seems to be in order,' Fraser replied. 'If anything else comes up that you think needs doing, Mother, I would be really happy if you let me know. I hate to think of you managing things like this on your own.'

She smiled. 'What a comfort you are to me,' she said. 'Margaret sorts me out very efficiently, but I don't feel very comfortable during the process. I don't know why – I know she means well. Let's have some lunch now. I'm feeling a bit tired. Celia bought some nice ham, and some cheese and rolls for us. Will that be enough for you?'

'Certainly it will.' He worried that she was looking pale. 'Don't you move. I'll bring it in. At least my culinary skills won't be put to the test, which is just as well. I'd no idea there was such a knack to cooking sausages. I burnt mine horribly.'

'You must have had the heat up too high.'

'Yes, I know that now. Everyone else seems to have got there ahead of me.'

He carried the lunch in, and helped her up to the table. He was horrified at the smallness of the portion she took, and was aware that although her knife and fork were quite busy on the plate, very little seemed to be getting conveyed to her mouth.

When he had cleared lunch away he asked her what the other thing she wanted to tell him was.

'I wanted to show you some old photos,' she said, 'and some papers. But oh dear, Fraser, I'm so sorry. I feel rather tired. I don't think I can manage it. Perhaps if I just have a little sleep first.' She looked distressed and suddenly very old. Fraser sat her in her chair and gently placed her blanket over her lap.

'There, mother, there's nothing to worry about. Nothing at all. You just have a rest, and we won't try to do anything more today. I'll leave you in peace now, but I'll tell you what I'll do. I'll come again next weekend, next Saturday - I promise. You try and rest over the next few days, and we can do everything you want then. Will that be alright?'

'Oh, could you really? Are you sure you have the time? I'm so sorry. Fraser. So very sorry.'

'Nothing to be sorry for,' he replied, kissing her gently. 'Just rest, and I'll see you again very soon. Goodbye for now, and look after yourself.'

'Goodbye, darling Fraser,' she said. 'Goodbye.'

Chapter 7

Joanna did not wake up early on Monday morning, which was hardly surprising as she had not set her alarm clock the night before. What was the point? With no job to provide an incentive it was not easy to summon up the enthusiasm to start another day. It was a vicious circle, really, because she lacked the motivation to look for a job, and without a job there was no real reason to function on all cylinders first thing in the morning.

The trouble was, she thought, it wasn't easy deciding which sort of job to go for. Up to now she'd managed to have enough income not to have to bother immediately – giving her plenty of time to think about it. That source had now, of course, dried up, forcing her to think again. Should she just look for something to fill in for a bit, or should she seriously consider getting on the rung of some sort of career ladder? If so, which ladder?

If university had worked out she might have had a better idea of where she was going. She'd had a problem deciding what sort of course to do – one she simply enjoyed for the content's sake – in which case she would have accepted Manchester's offer to study history – or a vocational one –

such as journalism at City University. She did love history, but on the other hand she'd fancied making her way in journalism. It might be fun to be out in some foreign war-torn land, reporting back to people at home – the sounds of gunfire in the background ensuring a dramatic effect, the heat and dust contrasting starkly with Britain's continual rain. Perhaps that was a pipe dream - and her mother's comments had not helped. They'd only heightened the indecision. She still smarted at the memory. Being told you were a useless parasite scarcely boosted the ego.

Because she had dithered for too long she had missed the university application deadlines, and so at the last minute took what was offered – i.e. reading English at Sussex, but she had found it difficult to settle, and wished she'd done the course at Manchester. She'd much have preferred that, she thought. By the time it came to the exams at the end of the first year she knew she had not done enough work to pass, so she dropped out and arrived home just when her fellow students were opening their exam papers.

Since then she had done a few odd jobs of one sort and another, and usually left before she could get fired. What she needed was some way of scouring the locality looking for a good job. That meant a car – and she had thought she was home and dry on that when the totally unexpected had happened.

Now she thought of her father and wondered if he would fall for this one. It was worth a try, and if she played her cards well, who knows? He was always kind, even if a bit disapproving at times, never grasping the real issues – in her view. She was rather reluctant to approach him when he was still obviously feeling his loss deeply, and she felt daunted at the thought. Sarah always seemed to know what to say, no matter what the situation, but she never did. Perhaps it would be good to give him a ring, anyway, and she could then see what the possibilities were, once the conversation had got underway.

Joanna rang Fraser's office number.

'Hi Dad, how are you?'

'I'm all right, thank you Joanna. I'm glad to hear from you. I was just saying to Granny yesterday that I hadn't spoken to you recently.'

'How was Granny?' Joanna asked

'She seemed very tired. She had said she wanted to show me some things – papers and photos – but in the end she didn't have the energy. So I said I'd go again next weekend and that seemed to please her.'

'What sort of papers?' asked Joanna.

'I've really no idea. But obviously something is on her mind.'

'You're very good to Granny,' said Joanna.

'Well, it's up to children to look after their parents, especially when they get elderly.'

'I don't do much for you,' Joanna replied with unusual honesty.

'That's perfectly true,' said Fraser. 'Fortunately, I am not elderly yet, so at the moment the boot is usually on the other foot. Why are you ringing? Is there something I can do for you?'

'I thought you might like to meet me this evening for a meal, for a change. There, you see, I do think of you sometimes.'

'Why do you want to? Is there a particular reason?' Fraser was fairly sure that by the end of the evening he would be dipping into his pocket. Joanna usually had ulterior motives.

'There's something I'd like to discuss with you. How about the Smugglers Arms at seven o'clock?'

'Very well, if you wish. So, how are you? Is James still around?'

'Good heavens, no! He disappeared long ago.'

'You're very good of getting rid of your boyfriends,' said Fraser. 'I suppose there's another one on the scene now.'

'Well, yes, actually there is.' Joanna's voice had gone a bit dreamy.

'Am I going to meet him? Are you bringing him this evening?'

'Certainly not,' said Joanna. 'Anyway, you wouldn't approve.'

'I suppose he's an escaped convict this time.'

'Not at all – he's very clever.'

'So what does he do?'

'Something in computers – not sure what, really.'

'You mean like Michael? Running his own business?'

'Rather like Michael, yes.'

'You're not telling me much about him. What's so great about him?'

'He's very good in bed,' said Joanna.

'I don't want to know that. Just tell me why I'm not going to approve.'

'Well,' said Joanna hesitantly, 'he's a… a Pakistani.'

'Oh, Joanna!' Fraser exploded. 'You really do know how to pick them! You're not going to marry this one, are you?'

'I doubt that very much,' she replied.

Fraser couldn't help feeling relieved. He knew she thought he had old-fashioned ideas, but a mixed marriage of that nature was not something he was going to find it easy to accept.

Joanna said, 'I expect he'll go back to his family in the end.'

'You mean back to Pakistan?'

'Something like that,' she replied. 'Anyway, see you this evening.'

She had chosen the most expensive item on the menu – knowing he would offer to pick up the tab at the end – and she was downing a gin and tonic.

'What about a job? Any progress?' he asked.

'That's what I wanted to talk to you about. I've decided the problem is I don't really know enough about the businesses in this locality. I mean, you can read adverts – but you have to go to a place to know if it's the sort of thing that would appeal – absorb the ambience – you know, that sort of thing. And I can't get round easily, because I've no transport of my own.'

The penny dropped. 'So you want me to buy you a car!'

'You can see how it would multiply the possibilities one hundredfold. And it would transform my life – it's so horrid having to come back at night from places on the underground – or by bus. Probably isn't at all safe, these days.'

'It's a pretty big thing to ask for. Most people have to work in order to afford one. You want it the other way round.'

'Oh please Dad – it would be so nice. And it would only be a loan. I'll pay you back as soon as I've got the money.'

Fraser wondered just how many times he'd heard that before – and how often he'd fallen for it - before it finally dawned that she had no intention of paying him back.

'I'm sorry, Joanna,' he said. 'I don't believe in young

people having everything handed to them on a plate. I've had to work my way up, and you must learn to do the same. Sarah has never asked for anything – she's earned everything she's got.'

Joanna could see this approach wasn't getting anywhere. But she had another card up her sleeve. It would have to emerge slowly, as he wasn't going to like it.

'Dad,' she said, 'can I ask – did Mummy make a will?'

Fraser pulled a face. 'No, I'm afraid not. I tried to persuade her to, and had my solicitor come round one day, but she was adamant, and refused. I did mine, but she had some sort of superstitious blockage about it, and wouldn't do it. Why do you ask?'

'Have you cleared up all her papers now?'

'I haven't touched them,' Fraser admitted. 'I got someone from one of those charities to come and take away all her clothes and bags, and scarves – that sort of thing. I couldn't bear seeing the dresses hanging in the wardrobe - they reminded me too much of her. She loved new clothes, and always looked so nice.'

'But you haven't looked at any of her personal documents?'

'No – Edie liked her areas of privacy, and one of these was where she kept all the important personal things. She used the bureau in the spare bedroom, and kept it locked. I was a bit surprised that she wanted to do this, as I was always quite open with her, but there seemed to be something in her nature that needed to do it that way, so I just let her arrange things as she wished. I have no idea what is in there, but I suppose all her financial documents, certificates, and all that kind of thing.'

'Don't you think you should sort it out now? I could

help you, if you like. I realise it's going to be painful for you. By the way, what happens to her money if she didn't make a will?'

'I did ask about this, although I never for a moment dreamt that she would go before me. I was always anxious to make sure she was provided for. I started giving her sums of money quite early in our marriage - as soon as I had some to spare - for her to put into a Savings Account, so that she could build up something of a nest egg over the years. I suppose that's all still there, in her name. It seems that, as her husband, surviving her, the law of intestacy means that it passes to me. But what's all this sudden interest in your mother's affairs?'

'Mother told me she would buy me a car. She'd been giving me some sums of money, knowing I didn't have a job yet, and she could see a car was a good idea, so she promised me one – only a few days before she ... before she died.'

Fraser choked over his mouthful of food. 'Your mother! Gave you money! Promised to buy you a car! Why ever would she do that?'

'Hush ...' said Joanna. 'I mean, you're shouting.'

'I'm sorry but you've made me angry. Just tell me why on earth your mother would have offered to buy you a car!'

'Perhaps she felt she wanted to, for some reason.'

'What rubbish. I don't know why she should even consider it for a moment - certainly not without discussing it with me. We did everything together. We always knew everything about each other.'

'Oh, Dad!' Pent up feelings were rushing to the surface. Joanna knew this wasn't the time or the place but she couldn't stop herself. 'You've gone around all your life with your eyes closed! How can you be so blind! I know you're going to tell me next that Mother was the best wife and mother in the world!'

'So she was!' Fraser could not contain his emotions either. 'You and Sarah were very lucky – she went to endless trouble to look after you girls – nothing was too much effort. She taught you all you needed to know in life – I don't ever want to hear you find fault with your mother. You've everything to be grateful to her for … everything!'

'Tell me this.' Joanna's voice was carefully controlled. 'Why do you think Sarah has to have her tight schedules? Why must she always have planned ahead for the next hour, the next day, the next week – but has no idea how to live in the present? Those poor kids have little scope for spontaneity or creativity – she's afraid they might make a mess, and she hasn't allowed enough time to clear it up! And why does she keep Michael on such a short leash? He's tried to be a good husband but she never gives him any quality time – and he deserves so much more – he's a loving, affectionate man and he needs to have someone to really love him and make a fuss of him. But Sarah's on an express train rushing into the distance, with no time ever to stop and enjoy anything on the way.'

Fraser couldn't believe what he was hearing. 'And you?' he asked. 'I suppose you'll say next that you know where you're going!'

'I haven't even got on any train yet,' she replied, 'because I can't decide which one to take. I'm a disappointment, aren't I? Come on, admit it, for once in your life. I can't make decisions, I can't settle on a career – I can't keep boyfriends more than five minutes. Think about it, and now tell me mother was the best mother in the world.'

'And you're claiming your mother is responsible for your shortcomings?'

'Mother was so burdened by her own lack of a sense of self worth that she loaded her hang-ups onto us. We were brought up with some nebulous goal ahead for which we had to strive to gain her approval. Sometimes she was lavish with praise – at other times heavy with disapproval – and our problem was we didn't really know what elicited which reaction. The goal posts kept moving. What was good one day wasn't the next. I think there was something buried deep inside her, perhaps when she was a child, that gave her a great big guilt complex, and she had to show the world that she had every reason to deserve its approval, with her idyllic marriage, her praiseworthy children, and her own personal beauty and charm.'

'So when did you gain a qualification in psychology? Your mother, having hang-ups, and a guilt complex – what utter nonsense!'

Fraser's face was white. Joanna had started and now she couldn't stop. 'You were always so thrilled with her, but deep down she believed she wasn't worthy of your unwavering admiration, so she kept pushing you to see how far she could go. She wanted there to be a ceiling, but there never was one. She behaved outrageously and you went on shutting you eyes to any fault in her, or in us, for that matter. She treated you abominably, and you let her get away with it.'

Fraser pushed his plate away. He sat back in his chair, his face pale and taut. After a little while he said, 'You're talking rot. Your mother always acted out of the best possible motives – all she wanted was that Sarah and you grew up to make the best of yourselves, to be happy, and to make your mother, and me, proud of you.'

'It wasn't that simple – Sarah and I were put under continual pressure but it was hopeless trying to say anything to you. You always got cross with us if you thought we'd upset her and you always supported her.'

Fraser spoke through clenched teeth. 'If you believe your mother promised you a car, then I will make good her promise. But I don't ever want to hear you speak like that about her again, especially now she...' He did not know how to finish the sentence. 'I'll get John to find you the cheapest car possible that's reliable – he seems to have a lot of contacts – and that will be the end of the matter. I never want to hear anything like this again. And I don't want any more to eat. Here's the money – you pay the bill. I'm going home.'

Not trusting himself to say any more, he left. He felt shattered. His family simply did not have rows or conflict. The idea that his children were not leading fulfilled and happy lives was incomprehensible. As for the indictment of Edie – he could not come to terms with it. The pain he now experienced was quite different from the pain of loss – that was understandable, at least. But this – he now felt thoroughly disturbed and did not know what to do with himself. Once home he walked round and round, wishing he could think of someone to ring up, so that he could talk and somehow rid himself of the unfamiliar and distressing feelings that were engulfing him – but he couldn't think of anyone.

Chapter 8

Her mother wore the familiar anxious look she never seemed to shed these days. If she wasn't looking tense and worried, she was usually in tears. This may have become the norm, but it didn't make it any easier for Angela to bear. Gone were the days of the happy smile which had made the world feel a good place. Doreen had been like this ever since that frightful day two years ago, now so deeply etched in Angela's memory.

Until then life had been relatively easy and comfortable for Angela, and Peter – her brother older by two years. Their father Maurice made a reasonable living, first as a taxi driver, and then, for several years now, as the private driver of an important government official. This meant that he worked long and unpredictable hours, was on call all the time, and was often away for nights as well as days. As a result their mother could devote much of her time to her children, and they felt well cared for and loved. The three of them formed a close bond.

One day when Angela was fourteen years old they were all on a shopping spree, and had naturally found their way to the large department store Doreen liked to frequent. She was a clever seamstress and made many of the clothes she and Angela wore. They were standing at the haberdashery counter while she chose buttons. The helpful sales assistant had brought out several trays, and Doreen was happily going from one to another, enjoying their feel, and colours and shapes.

Suddenly Peter spun round and fell to the floor, foaming at the mouth, his body jerking convulsively. A small crowd gathered round, and a supervisor rushed up to investigate the commotion. Shoppers craned their necks to see what was going on. An ambulance was called, and Peter was carried out on a stretcher, still shaking and jerking. Angela never lost the memory of the feeling of fear she experienced at Peter's strange behaviour – her brother seemed to have been transformed into an alien being, and she thought he would die.

The diagnosis was epilepsy – or 'grand mal' as people called it. Drugs were used to treat it but they were not successful in controlling the fits completely. From that day on Doreen became more and more anxious. The symptoms were completely unpredictable. Peter would be perfectly normal one moment, and the next he would be on the ground, rolling about and jerking, often making strange noises. Sometimes when he fell he would knock himself on objects, and end up with a number of bruises. Once he had a fit while carrying a glass, which smashed as he fell and cut him badly. It became difficult to go anywhere, and it seemed best he left school, as in any case he was now sixteen. So Doreen kept him mostly at home, and although friends came to see him, some were frightened off by the fits, and started coming less frequently.

There was still a certain amount of stigma attached

to the disease. From early days it had been considered somehow connected with devils, and those who suffered from it often tried to keep it a secret. The transformation of the sufferer into a writhing, inhuman being was frightening to those who had no understanding of what was actually happening, and in biblical times many believed that the sufferer was possessed by demons.

Although Peter's education came to an abrupt end Angela was doing well at school, and was encouraged to consider a university place. She longed to do this, as books had become important to her, but she realised her mother would find it difficult if she went away. However, Maurice was adamant that Angela's life should not be spoiled as a result of her brother's illness, and Doreen, to her credit, agreed. Angela could hardly believe her good fortune when she was granted a place at Bristol University where she had opted to read Classics.

Life at University suited Angela well. She loved the Wills Memorial Building with its tower rising up over the city. She was thrilled by the imposing entrance, her spirits always lifting as she climbed the wide stone stairs leading up to the Great Hall and the Lecture rooms. She spent hours in the Library between lectures, engrossed in her private study, and the terms flew by. She made friends among the undergraduates, both male and female, and joined various societies. However, it was not her intention to become involved in any deep relationships, as she felt a strong sense of duty towards her family, and spent her vacations doing her best to help and comfort her mother, who was struggling to keep her spirits up in the face of the continuing problems with Peter.

Having successfully progressed through her course,

Angela now faced her final examinations. She knew she had prepared as thoroughly as she possibly could, and felt fairly confident. At the end of the second day she was called to the telephone. Peter had had a brain haemorrhage and had died. Her mother, although in a state of great distress, begged her to finish all her examination papers before she came home. Somehow Angela managed to keep her focus on what she was doing, and delayed succumbing to the grief she felt until she had written the last paper. Then she crumpled on her bed and sobbed out her anguish for some time, before collecting herself to pack and come home for the funeral.

Doreen never recovered from this loss. She sank into a deep depression, which Maurice did not know how to handle. He took to being away for longer periods.

Angela's results were good – she had achieved upper second class honours, narrowly missing a first. Her course, however, whilst providing the discipline of study, had not fitted her out for any particular career. She had given considerable thought to this, and became and more and more attracted to the idea of finding out how people's minds worked, and how you could help those who were suffering from some form of mental illness, such as her mother. Wisely, however, she realised she needed to mature and experience life more fully herself before she would be in a position to help others. What she needed was a stopgap, and she found this in the idea of being a librarian. To spend her days amongst books appealed strongly, and would give her the opportunity of reading more widely. She trained as a librarian, qualified, and found a job near home, so that she could continue to support her mother.

Before she had begun her new job her mother was

rushed to Charing Cross Hospital with heart trouble. Her blood pressure had, over the years, become increasingly high, and she suffered a major heart attack. At the hospital there was a brilliant heart surgeon who was making a worldwide reputation for himself, pioneering new techniques which attracted young and newly qualified surgeons eager to learn from the best.

One of these was the American surgeon Martin Makoni, who was a rising star in New York, and who acted as assistant in Doreen's case. In fact it was he who performed the surgery, under the watchful eye of his mentor, and it was said that he had done an extremely good job. Doreen's condition, however, continued to give cause for concern.

Angela had been on the point of taking up her post as librarian, but when her mother became ill she had to ask for a postponement, knowing this would probably mean that she would lose the job. She spent a great deal of her time either sitting in a small waiting room, or beside her mother, waiting for developments. Martin often came to speak to her, updating her with the latest situation, and sometimes just engaging her in conversation, finding out a little of her background, and being generally kind and sympathetic. Then, one day, to Angela's surprise, he asked her out for dinner. He explained that he was in London on a two year secondment, and as he put in long hours at the hospital he had little opportunity to make any social contacts. Angela accepted the invitation, and found him charming company with an ease of communication and a sensitive nature that warmed her. He was eight years older than she was, and his maturity was attractive. As he described his mission – to save as many lives as he could by repairing broken bodies - she felt that this paralleled her own desire to try and assist with the healing of broken minds and spirits. She spent two more evenings with him, each time finding depths that pleased her, and to her own surprise she greatly enjoyed his company.

Then, one evening, as she sat beside her mother, she became aware that there were warning lights on the monitors. Nurses began to rush in and out, and asked her to go and sit in the waiting room. Martin came to find her, and explained that her mother was undergoing a crisis and they would were doing everything they could. She sat there, feeling numb, for three more hours. Then she looked up at the sound of someone coming in and saw Martin standing there, his face grim.

'I'm so sorry,' he said. 'We tried everything, but it was no good.' Angela thanked him, and then began to weep. He sat down beside her and put his arm round her. He did not say anything further, but waited patiently while she struggled to compose herself. When she had done so she stood up, and he took her arm to see her off the premises.

'I'll be in touch,' he said, 'regarding the arrangements. I have your telephone number. I'll be in touch.'

Angela's days had been completely filled with the hospital visiting so that she suddenly found herself at a loss to know what to do. She began to think about her future, and decided to try and pursue the librarian job, which had been on hold all this time.

Then Martin had rung, and once again they had met for an evening together. She found his strength and understanding comforting, but she certainly wasn't expecting him to ask her to marry her. When he did, she was even more surprised to hear herself accept, without hesitating for a moment, although he had explained it would mean living in America. There were no ties to prevent her from pursuing her own life any more – she had lost her mother, and her father, it transpired, had long been finding his solace elsewhere, and had no need of her. With Peter gone as well, it suddenly seemed a very appealing idea to start a new life in a new continent – and with a new husband!

Angela enjoyed the excitement of settling down and getting used to a different country and environment. Martin had proudly told her about the hospital where he worked, Mount Sinai Hospital, Fifth Avenue, New York - one of the oldest and largest teaching hospitals in America. Apparently, when it was founded in 1855, it was called 'The Jews' Hospital', as Sampson Simpson, the philanthropist who founded it, wanted to provide for the needs of the growing Jewish immigrant community. However, some eleven years later, as it became an integral part of the community, its name was changed to 'The Mount Sinai Hospital' so that it would be free of any racial or religious distinction. In the twentieth century, as the population of New York exploded, the hospital was in increasing demand and this was a time of great expansion. In recent years it had gained a tremendous reputation, and became a 'surgery Centre of Excellence'. No wonder Martin was proud to be a surgeon there, where many heart conditions were treated.

They had an apartment on West 77th Street, and Martin had a short drive across Central Park to work. He was anxious that his new wife should be happy, and took her to meet his colleagues – who, she quickly discovered, held him in high regard, and she made the acquaintance of his large family, by whom she was warmly welcomed and quickly accepted.

Martin knew that to be happy she must be occupied, and they had often discussed the way she wanted her life to go, so he set about finding the most suitable course where she could gain a qualification. The idea of embarking on study again, this time of a vocational nature, appealed to her greatly. She would meet people of like mind, and feel that she was progressing towards an objective. They settled on the M.A. course in Counselling for Mental Health and Wellness at New York University.

Angela could not believe how happily life had turned out for her. She had a husband whose ideals she admired, and whose likeable personality made him a joy to live with. Meanwhile she worked hard and delighted in all the new insights she was gaining. No one could have been prouder than Martin when she graduated, and subsequently found a post in a Mental Health Center, where she could now use all her skills.

If there was a disappointment, it was that no children had arrived on the scene. After realising that this wasn't proving straightforward they took tests, and it came to light that the glandular fever Martin had suffered from as a teenager had rendered him infertile. After feeling sad about this initially they both decided they must take the positive view, and see all the people they cared for over the years as substitute children.

Twenty years had passed since they had married. Martin wanted to celebrate – he never lost his romantic side, and as they discussed it the evening before he looked at her with such tenderness that her heart felt it would burst. He loved to surprise her, so all he would say was, 'Be sure you are ready, looking as wonderful as always, at six o'clock. I will be home as soon after that as I possibly can.'

'What if you get an emergency in?' she asked.

'Don't worry, honey' he said. 'I've made contingency

plans, and set up a back stop. If the Queen of England was brought in needing immediate heart surgery she would be told 'You'll have to make do with someone else – Martin Makoni has an engagement he will not break!' Nothing is going to stop me coming back for you tomorrow evening. And I'm going on the town with the most beautiful woman in the world – you just watch!'

She had made sure she had no commitments the next day, and could attend to her preparations in a relaxed way. In the morning the doorbell rang and an enormous bunch of flowers was delivered. In the afternoon there was another ring – this time a large bottle of champagne. She smiled to herself, thinking that no woman should be this happy – she really was the luckiest person alive.

She was all ready in her new red dress – she knew the deep colour set off her dark hair beautifully. She was lucky that, although in her early fifties now, there were only a few grey streaks – she still had an amazing head of thick dark hair. Just before 6 pm. she had a call from him. He often used his mobile phone to tell her he was on his way. He was just crossing Central Park.

'Is my beautiful wife all ready for her amazing night out? I'll be back real soon.' Then his voice changed. 'What the devil! Hang on a moment honey.' She heard the car stop. He must have got out, because she could hear a woman screaming – strange terrified cries, hysterical, almost like an animal. Then she heard shouting, men's voices. She thought she heard Martin's, but it was muffled, she couldn't be sure. Phrases, jumbled, mixed with the loud screaming, came down the phone - 'Get away!', 'Leave her alone!', and 'Beat it, nigger!' There were sounds of a scuffle, and another cry – this time a man's. Suddenly it all went quiet. Then

Martin's voice, so soft she could scarcely hear him, 'Angie, honey, come quickly, in the Park. I'm hurt.'

She ran, as fast as she could, all the time holding the phone to her ear, repeating, 'I'm coming, Martin, hang on, I'm coming!'

A little knot of people were gathered round a figure on the ground. She raced up and the crowd fell back to give her room. She fell on her knees beside him, and saw the pool of blood. With her face pressed up against his she sobbed, 'Martin, are you all right? Oh, Martin, darling!'

'I'm so sorry, Angie, honey,' he was crying as he tried to speak, 'I'm so sorry.'

Someone in the crowd said an ambulance had been called. Others were talking about a girl, a retarded girl, who was being attacked by two youths.

The paramedics arrived and she moved back to let them attend to Martin. They were fast, efficient, and obviously very concerned. He was taken away on a stretcher and Angie went with them in the Ambulance back to Mount Sinai, where a team had been alerted and were poised for action. They raced with him to the theatre, and Angela found herself in a waiting room, in an agony of suspense.

The police came to visit her. They had collected witness statements. It seemed that Martin had seen the harassment by two youths of a twenty-year-old girl with Down's Syndrome. The girl was walking back from work across the park, when these youths had spotted her as fair game, and were making lewd suggestions, putting their arms round her, and forcing themselves on her. She was terrified, and had started screaming. Martin had been passing at that moment, and with his medical background he would instantly have recognised the features of this short, rather squat girl with slightly flattened face and upward slanting eyes. He could not bear to see someone so vulnerable becoming prey to the cruel treatment of these young men, and true to his nature he had to try and help. One of the men must have had a knife, for Martin had been stabbed in the back.

Angela sat there for what seemed hours. A policewoman sat with her, but Angela was hardly aware of her. From time to time someone would come from the theatre to say that he was still alive, but only just. They were working very hard to save him.

Then the surgeon in charge came. He stood there, unable to say anything. He didn't need to, because Angela knew. Martin, who had fought so hard to save the lives of countless others, had lost his own battle. Instead of the evening of pure joy they had both anticipated so eagerly the world had changed and turned black. Angela sat and wept.

Chapter 9

The curtains were drawn although it was early afternoon, and in the darkened bedroom Sarah was lying curled up on her bed, cursing the searing pain that seemed to be splitting her head in two as her temple throbbed incessantly. This could not be happening! She simply could not afford to waste time having a migraine. As it was she had had to cancel two meetings and arrange for her other tasks to be carried out by her already hard-pressed colleague so that she could leave the office. Driving back had been a nightmare as she could scarcely concentrate on the road ahead and felt blinded by the pain.

Thank goodness the children would not be home until 5.30 pm, and thank goodness also that today Laura would be collecting them from the after-school playgroup and bringing them back.

She had three hours to get over this monster of a headache – but at the moment it showed no sign of abating. She had been succumbing to them more frequently recently, but usually she could carry on working, gritting her teeth and waiting for the pain killers to work. Today's affliction was different. The agonising pain had the upper hand and she was powerless to fight it. What's more she felt nauseous.

She clutched her head and rolled to and fro, moaning as she simply tried to survive the next wave of agony, waiting for the tablets she had taken to work. Fortunately she had stocked up a few weeks ago on some especially strong ones the chemist had recommended, although he had advised her, at the same time, that if the headaches persisted she should see her doctor. As if she had time for visiting doctors! It would go, she was sure, if she could only hang on long enough.

She heard a key in the door – Michael did sometimes come home in the day time between visits. He would know she was here as her car was outside, and she heard him calling her name. There were footsteps on the stairs and then he opened the bedroom door.

'Sarah! What is it? Are you ill?'

He sat down on the edge of the bed and she clasped his hand tightly between hers and pressed it to her forehead. The tears began to trickle down her cheeks. She felt her control slipping away. The next moment she got up quickly and rushed into the bathroom where she vomited violently.

He followed her speaking gently, and coaxed her back to bed. He cleared up in the bathroom where she had missed the toilet, and brought her a glass of water to take the horrible taste out of her mouth.

'Just lie down,' he said, 'and don't worry about anything. I'll see to whatever needs to be done. Is there anything urgent in the next hour or so? What about the twins?'

She explained that they would be brought back, and it was just their tea that had to be prepared. It felt comforting to lean on him. She always seemed to be the one at the forefront, directing proceedings, seeing that all the wheels ran smoothly, that all the arrangements were quite clear, and everyone knew what the plans were.

'Are you going out again?' she asked.

'I had a visit booked,' he replied, 'but I won't go. I'm not going to leave you. I want you to lie there very quietly and try to sleep. I think you have been pushing yourself too hard recently. You simply must slow down.'

'I'm sorry to be a nuisance,' she said, 'and I'm sure I'll be fine soon, but thank you, Michael. The pain has lessened – I think I could sleep now.'

As he went downstairs she heard his mobile phone ring. She did not hear what he said but he seemed to be having a difficult time. Perhaps it was not all that easy to get out of his next visit - his voice was raised, and he sounded angry. Then everything went quiet and she drifted into a healing sleep.

Joanna hoped she had created a dreamy, romantic setting in her bedroom. To exclude the bright, day time light she had partially drawn her curtains, and in the background gentle music was coming from her CD player. On the table was a bottle of champagne on ice and two glasses, heady perfume was in the air, and she lay languidly on the bed, wearing only her silk negligee. She settled down to wait.

He had said he would be able to come this afternoon. He had promised. There might be a whole two hours together of blissful love-making. She longed to hear him ring the doorbell. She waited.

As the time went on she began to get irritated. Where was he? She knew delays could occur but now frustration was setting in. She decided to ring. If there was another excuse she did not know how she would stand it.

She cut off the call, and with a face like thunder, hurled her mobile phone at the wall where it thudded with an ominous sound and then lay in two pieces on the floor. Sobbing hysterically she threw herself face down on the bed and gave full vent to her fury and disappointment.

Chapter 10

Where had he put that scrap of paper? Fraser scrabbled through the pockets of the jacket he thought he had worn to the party, but to no avail. He tried the trouser pockets – and in the end searched through every pair hanging there, although he was sure he knew which ones he had worn that evening.

He sat down feeling annoyed and frustrated. It had suddenly come to him where he could go for help – hadn't she said something about if he should need an ear to bend? – but now he was powerless to pursue the idea. He supposed he could ring Margaret and ask her to phone Marion for Angela's number, but that was the last thing he wanted to do. Margaret would be her usual nosy self and want to know why he wanted it. He could see her secretly rubbing her hands at the thought that he was about to ask Angela for a date – and congratulating herself for getting him out to that party.

A remote possibility occurred to him. He got up to fetch his wallet, opened it, and there, tucked in the corner was the little piece of paper.

That was one hurdle overcome, but this was immediately

followed by another huge one. What would he say? He certainly didn't want her to get the wrong idea. And what on earth was he doing passing some of his family woes on to a complete stranger? The funny thing was – she hadn't seemed like a complete stranger last Saturday evening. She had seemed somehow familiar; it was as if the usual barriers when it came to getting to know someone new weren't there. He must be imagining that. This was a really bad idea. Fraser screwed the paper up into a ball and tossed it at the waste paper bin. It missed, and lay on the floor, seeming to look at him and say, 'What are you frightened of? Come on, pick me up and make that call.'

Well, if it was only a matter of his own pain, he could cope. He certainly wouldn't bother Angela with that. He may have been suffering, but it had been a comfort to him to think that at least his two daughters were happy and fulfilled, and he had two lovely grandchildren as well. But now it seemed as if everything he'd believed in and treasured was disintegrating – that nothing was as he had thought.

He retrieved the piece of paper, unrolled it, and without allowing himself to delay any longer, dialled the number. It rang and then clicked on to the answerphone. He was about to hang up when he found himself saying, 'It's Fraser. We met at Marion's monstrous party and you were kind enough to give me your telephone number. Something has recently come up and I was wondering if I could take advantage of your kind offer and speak to you. But I don't want to bother you. Please don't worry if you're too busy. It's quite all right.' He left his phone number and rang off, feeling rather stupid.

Five minutes later his phone rang.

'Hello,' said Angela. 'Sorry I missed your call. I've just come in from shopping. How are you?'

'Feeling rather confused and silly,' said Fraser. 'I shouldn't have troubled you. I have a few family traumas and I remembered that you encouraged me to feel free to contact you. But now that I've done so I'm wondering why on earth you should be in any way interested in the Coleman goings on.'

'Actually,' she replied, 'I'm glad you've phoned. To tell you the truth, I'm at a bit of a loose end just now, as I've a few 'goings on' myself that I'm waiting to have cleared up. And I'm inordinately interested in other people – it's a lifelong habit I can't seem to break - so I'd be very pleased to spend a little time, if you will allow it, listening to anything you like to tell me. Do you want to speak on the phone or shall we meet up? I'm free for the rest of the day if you can spare the time.'

He was a little taken aback – he hadn't quite visualised things developing so quickly, but thought he might as well strike while the iron was hot.

'What about meeting for lunch,' he said. 'I know a pleasant little café near the river.'

'That sounds a great idea. And then we can go for a walk and you can talk as much or as little as you want. I'll see you there.'

An hour and a half later they were seated in the small café enjoying a rather well cooked first course. He had gone for an old favourite – liver and bacon - and she was having baked cod and vegetables. They had done the pleasantries, and now Fraser was feeling rather awkward. What had he let himself in for? He had no idea what to say or how to begin. But Angela seemed perfectly relaxed and at ease. She said, 'Has something new happened?'

'I'm feeling slightly shell shocked,' he said. 'These last seven weeks I've been bitterly regretting the loss of my wife after 31 years of the happiest possible marriage, but at least I've found comfort in the fact that our two daughters enjoyed all the benefits of being brought up by their very special mother. Sarah, the older girl, seems to have everything now – a good husband, two lovely children and a thriving business, and I felt it was only a matter of time before Joanna found her way forward and started to make something of herself. Then I have this astonishing conversation with her when she seems to be accusing her mother of – oh, I don't know what – but somehow of being responsible for the misery both she and Sarah are experiencing. I had no idea they were – I thought they were both happy in their different ways.'

Angela continued to eat in silence.

'Oh, I can't do this,' said Fraser, feeling uncomfortable and not knowing how to go on. 'I'm so unused to delving into things. I've always taken the line that people know what's in their own best interests and who am I to interfere? The best thing I can do is leave them to get on with it. What do I know? I don't even know how to talk about it.'

'I tell you what,' said Angela. 'I can never resist desserts – I ought to, I know, but there you are. Let's choose one, and then we'll go outside and take a walk – and perhaps talking will be a bit easier.'

'I really don't know.' Fraser sat there shaking his head. 'You are very kind, but perhaps we'll finish our very nice meal and call it a day.'

He called for the menu and they both studied it. Then he became aware that Angela was stifling a noise. He looked up in surprise and saw her shoulders shaking – was she crying? No, there was a smile on her face and she seemed to be giggling.

'What is it?' he asked, beginning to smile a little himself, not knowing why, but simply because her laughter was infectious.

'Have you read the bottom of the menu?' she asked.

'Baked jam sponge and custard.'

'No - underneath that – right at the bottom, in small print.'

He looked closer and read out: "'Please be aware that we are working with nuts in our kitchen." Oh my goodness,' he said, 'what are they going to serve up, do you think? Upside Down Pudding?'

'Perhaps some kind of Fruit Fool. Rhubarb?

'Rhubarb.'

'No doubt topped with cracked wheat.'

By now they were both laughing, and suddenly Fraser felt a weight lifting from him.

'Look,' he said. 'I'm the nut, here. I've been handed a rather special opportunity to talk through some of my worries, and I'm such a coward I was on the point of throwing it away. I don't know why I feel it would be a relief to talk to you, but I do. Let's have our pudding and a cup of coffee, and then we'll go and walk it all off, and I'll try and bear my soul, if you can stand it – or at least that part which is concerning me at present.'

'That sounds a great plan,' she said. 'Well done.'

As they walked along by the river bank Fraser started to tell Angela what was troubling him.

'I've been so miserable at the loss of my beautiful Edie, but I thought that at least I could look back and be thankful for my marriage and two children who were privileged to have the best mother in the world. I believed they had their feet planted firmly on solid ground - but now it seems I've been deluding myself all these years. I was astonished at the way Joanna lashed out, and the things she said. I couldn't believe her bitterness and resentment.'

He went on to relate the events of that evening, when Joanna had asked for a car, and when he demurred, had claimed that Edie had been giving her money for some time, and had actually promised to buy her one.

'How did you respond?' Angela asked.

'Well, of course, I got a bit angry and must have raised my voice, because Joanna told me to be quiet. Then out came the accusations – that Edie had had 'hang-ups' and a 'guilt complex' and had put such pressures on the two of them with the result that they are now - what's the word? – dysfunctional.'

He outlined a picture of Sarah putting her family under pressure with her strategies of military precision, and he passed on the analogy Joanna had used of the express train. Then there were Joanna's problems, the way she was riddled with indecision, and getting nowhere. But what had hurt him most were the statements about Edie – he could hardly bear to repeat them – but did manage to get out the bit about 'used him abominably' and 'behaved outrageously'.

Angela was quiet for a while. Then she said, 'I'm very glad you telephoned. You have had an awful lot thrown at you in a very short space of time. It does help if you can share some of it.'

'I shouldn't have involved you,' said Fraser. 'I suppose I should really have contacted Margaret, but I didn't think

I could face some of her astringent comments. She never was Edie's number one fan – although they seemed to get on pretty well on the whole. And I couldn't possibly burden my poor darling mother – she's 85 and getting forgetful and very frail.'

'Can I ask you something?' said Angela. 'Do you think people are always what they seem?'

'I don't know,' he replied. 'I suppose so – well, I think people generally are. I'm pretty sure I am. I'm an uncomplicated sot of person. With me, what you see is what you get.'

'Yes, I imagine that's true, but I'm wondering if it's always the case with other people. Perhaps, sometimes, you get what you don't see?'

'I don't know how to answer that. This sort of talk isn't my forte. How can I know if I don't see something?'

'Sometimes what you've missed may be brought forcibly to your attention, and then it can be rather a shock. Do you think your daughters have picked up the same sort of approach to life that you have? Do they have your values?'

'I don't really know what my approach is, except that I like to do the right thing by people, and make as much of a success of my life as I can. How can I put it? Life, to me is like a kitchen. I look for a design that will be a good arrangement, provide everything that's needed in an efficient way, then I go about sorting out the parts, and then I install it, to the best of my ability, and there you are – home, wife, family, and a reasonable income – and that's it.'

'And then you live happily ever after?'

'Yes, for the most part, I have done. And I think Edie did too. I know she was moody, but that was just her temperament. When she was happy she was exhilarated –

delighted with herself and with life – and I always believed that things were good for her, on the whole.'

'I like your kitchen analogy. Just suppose, there happened to be a weak point in the basic fabric of the room which you didn't realise when you put all your nice new shiny surfaces in place, and for a long time everything's fine. But gradually the fault begins to make itself felt – perhaps a leak happens, and slowly the new fitments get contaminated, and become warped and twisted. What then? How would you deal with it?'

'Are you saying that I'm just papering over the cracks?'

'It's worth thinking about, in light of what you are now learning about your daughters. It could be that there has been some stuff going on under the surface that you weren't aware of, and this has now resulted in problems for your girls.'

'This is all a bit deep for me,' sighed Fraser. 'I'm not used to analysing things like this. I've always just taken them as they are.'

'As I see it you can do one of two things,' said Angela. 'You can set out on a voyage of discovery, which will involve some unfamiliar sights and experiences. Because the territory will be new you may be get worried, and there could well be some pain along the way, but in the end you will arrive at a place where you understand your daughters far better, are able to communicate with them on a deeper level, and perhaps even be a support in helping them through some of their difficulties. In the end you will feel better about yourself.'

'And the other option?'

'Bury your head in the sand and forget any of these things were said. Go on exactly as before, keeping the image of everyone that you have held up to now, and stand back while events move on to their logical conclusions. These may be negative for everyone concerned, perhaps even disastrous.'

'I don't know. I've always been a bit of a stick-in-the-mud.'

'It's your decision,' she said, 'but will you think about it? I know it's new and rather daunting, but I promise you one thing – I'll help where I can. I have had some experience in sharing people's problems.'

'Why should you do that for me? Until recently I was a stranger. And I know so little about you. Won't you tell me more about your situation? This all feels rather one-sided.'

'I will tell you in detail soon,' she said. 'As I've said my affairs are in a state of limbo at the moment. I'm waiting to be called back to the States, and I'm a little on edge until that happens. The waiting is hard, so I'm glad to be involved in a problem quite removed from my own, and I believe that because I can be objective, without any personal or emotional involvement, I can be some help to you, and that would actually be helping me too.'

'I will think about what you've said. I promise.'

'There's one thing I want to ask you. Have you wrapped up your wife's affairs?'

'It's funny you should say that. Joanna asked me if Edie had left a will, and although I'm pretty sure she didn't, I haven't looked through anything. I did get rid of all her clothes, but she kept her paperwork in a locked bureau, and I haven't had the heart, up to now, to go through it.'

'That's something you will have to do, one of these days, and if you don't mind me being there, I could come, when you feel you can do it. I needn't look at anything, but if it would give you a little more strength, I would be happy to do that.'

'Thank you,' he said. 'You really are very kind. I rather think that might help a lot.'

By now they were almost back to where they had left the cars.

'You have made me feel much better,' he said. 'I'll think about what you've said, and let you know. I realise what I should do, and what I must do where all the personal papers and so on are concerned. I'm going to see Mother on Saturday. After that I will be in touch.'

'Promise?' she asked, as he held the car door open for her to get in.

'Scout's Honour,' he said. 'Oh, there was something else Joanna said.'

She rolled her car window down and waited.

He leaned down to speak to her. 'Do you know, her latest boyfriend is a Pakistani!'

'And that's bad?' asked Angela.

'Well, it's obviously most unsuitable. She said I'd disapprove, and then she told me that.'

'And do you disapprove? She asked.

'Well,' said Fraser, 'the thing is …'

'Yes?' prompted Angela.

'The thing is…' said Fraser.

Angela waited.

'The thing is,' said Fraser vehemently, 'I hate Indian food!'

Chapter 11

She must try and be more organised this time. What a pity that when Fraser had come last week she had run out of energy. Marjorie regretted that growing old meant everything became a great effort. She had planned to tell him all sorts of things – things she should have dealt with a long time ago – but when it came to it she had simply not been able to do it.

Dear Fraser still seemed vulnerable. Here he was, a grown man and a grandfather, but she often saw the small boy who had come face to face with tragedy when he was very young, and who had had his world shattered. How could she have put all the facts before him then? He had already learned one of life's hardest truths – that it is the people we love the most who have the power to inflict the deepest pain. He had dealt with it by closing down the part of his mind that held the painful memories. He had pushed away the unwelcome facts, and tried to carry on as if nothing had happened. She had let him, because it seemed too cruel to do anything else. And yet she longed to say, 'Do you remember when you and Daddy planted those seeds? Do you remember how we all went on a picnic?'

Rightly or wrongly she had not done so, with the result that the subject of his father had become increasingly difficult to bring up.

And now she had left it almost too late. When he came this time she would tackle it straight away. She would show him the letters and the old photographs, and the certificates, and she would try to tell him as much as she knew.

But would she be able to remember everything when she needed to? That was another problem. Her deteriorating mind kept playing stupid tricks on her. How strange it was that she could close her eyes and see scenes from those early happy days, as clearly as if they had happened yesterday, and yet she frequently struggled to remember what she had been about to do, or why she had gone into the kitchen, or where she had put her glasses this time!

It wasn't surprising that her days felt disjointed because she kept falling asleep. She'd put on the television to watch Countdown, and it would be all over, and she hadn't seen any of it. She couldn't seem to stop her head falling forward, then her eyes closed, and she was off. Of course it was a different matter when she was in bed at night. Then she often tossed and turned for hours. But for some reason the day time passed in a series of dozes, some longer than others.

When did Fraser say he would come? She thought he had said Saturday. She wondered what day it was today, and decided she should get up and go and look at the calendar. She would do so in a minute. As soon as she felt a little stronger. And as soon as the nagging pain had died down. Meanwhile she would just sit there a little longer, just a few more minutes.

Her head drooped forwards, and she slid into unconsciousness once more.

Chapter 12

Michael had a puncture. It was most annoying because he was on his way to pick up the twins and this meant he would be late. The children were not allowed to go outside – quite rightly, as they were very young – and a teacher or carer always stayed until the last pupil had been collected. However, it wasn't a nice feeling to be the last parent to arrive on the scene. You were always eyed rather aggressively, and the question as to why you were late and had kept them waiting hung unspoken in the air.

He prided himself on being able to change a tyre quickly, but even so it was going to mean twenty minutes that he hadn't bargained for. And the spare didn't look too healthy. He should have kept a check on it, instead of leaving it until the need arose. But you always think these things aren't going to happen today, and then they do. He wondered if there was enough air in it to limp along to the nearest garage, which, of course, would add another five minutes to the time.

Suddenly he realised he was thinking like Sarah! Under her influence he seemed to be measuring out his days in valuable time slots which, once allocated, could not be changed without causing a major disruption.

When did she get like that? She wasn't when he had first married her. She had been fun, in those days. Now the fun element seemed to have evaporated, along, sadly, with much of the love-making, since she always appeared stressed. She kept him going on promises, such as, 'When we've got the new bathroom sorted out, with the extra shower, it will be a lot easier to get us all ready in the morning, and things won't be quite so frantic.' But they had been, because now the twins had to take additional things with them, since their day contained extra activities, and rounding up something that was missing put the mornings firmly back on the 'frantic' list once more.

He realised that they had got into a spiral, and couldn't see how to get out of it, or when things would calm down. He had been all in favour when Sarah had suggested having her own small business – but he had thought it would just be a part-time occupation, something for her to do working from home, that she could easily fit in during the day, and which would give her an interesting outlet for her energies. That's how it had started, but it had grown rather bigger and become all-encompassing, so that now she rented a small office and had an employee working for her. When the twins were babies she had used a baby-minding service, but now they were of school age the whole thing had got incredibly complicated. He did what he could, but he had his own computer enterprise, which fortunately was lucrative. This was just as well, since there seemed to be no end to the demands for money these days.

Michael felt stifled by it all, as the pressures squeezed tighter. What he needed was a breath of fresh air from time to time. Surely every chap had a right to that? He did not know how he would survive if he wasn't able to escape briefly every now and again. But it wasn't easy to manage it. And it was getting harder and harder.

The car wheel was changed. He must get some more air – and then face the wrath of whoever was looking after the twins today.

Chapter 13

That Saturday morning the sun was shining brightly, although, with the approach of Autumn, it brought little warmth. The leaves had a wonderful golden glow, marvellous to behold, but heralding to all who looked up that they were about to die. The seasons were moving on.

Fraser had set off early, wanting to arrive at his mother's house before she had a chance to get too tired. He had rung her the previous day to remind her that he was coming, and had found that she did know, and hoped to have everything ready for him. But her voice had sounded subdued, and the usual liveliness was missing. The call had left him with a worried feeling, and he was glad he was going to be seeing her that day.

Perhaps Margaret was right and it really was time she went into a care home so that she could be looked after properly. Then he suddenly had an idea. She could come and live with him! He could probably afford to have his place adapted for her needs – put in an extra bathroom – perhaps make a sort of little granny flat on the ground floor! Then he could engage some daily help to see to her needs, do some cleaning and cooking. Now that would be a great advantage – perhaps they might even know how to cook sausages! Of course, Margaret would help too, so everything wouldn't be entirely on his shoulders. He was warming to the idea, and wondered why he hadn't thought of it before. Honesty compelled him to admit that it would not have been a possibility when Edie was alive – there would have been too many difficulties to surmount. Edie would probably have resented all the thought and effort he would have had to put in for the arrangement to be possible, and then she wouldn't have liked him spending a lot of time with his mother. No, it would have been unthinkable before – but now …

He wondered why Edie had stopped coming with him in the later years when he went to visit Marjorie. For many years she used to accompany him on most of his visits, and Marjorie, as he would have expected, had swept her up in the warmest of welcomes and always showed great pleasure at seeing her. He could not really remember when the excuses had begun - perhaps it was about five or so years ago. Whenever he had told Edie he was planning to visit Marjorie, she would say she had a headache, or there were too many things she had to get finished, or she really needed to shop for an item that was urgently required. It took some time, because Edie was so convincing, before he realised that in fact she had no intention of coming any more, and he did not ask her why, for fear of upsetting her. Once, in a roundabout sort of way, he had tried to raise the subject with his mother, but she had simply replied that probably Edie had very good reasons, and did not seem offended about it. So Fraser had not pursued the matter.

A vague feeling of doubt was beginning to stir inside him. Had he been deluding himself all these years? He couldn't have been so mistaken, could he? It was true that Edie was, well, a bit moody, and he was never quite sure whether he would find the happy, laughing, attractive woman, full of vitality, who so fascinated him – or the unresponsive one who brushed aside his approaches and seemed to be engrossed with her own thoughts. But he had learned to ride these times out. He prided himself on knowing how to handle her. He was constant in his attitude towards her - always sunny and affectionate, knowing that before long she would revert to the loving wife who was so dear to him, and eventually she would reward his patience in ways that took his breath away.

In the days just before she died – it was still difficult to think those words, let alone say them – she had been at her scintillating best – bright, sparkling – a joy to watch and to be with. He could not believe that one cruel blow of fate had, in a matter of seconds, taken her away.

His mind dwelt on some of the many happy times – often they were when he had taken her away for a short break, or a holiday. He had always booked the best he could find so that she would be thoroughly pampered. Once the girls had grown up and they were free to go away together, they had travelled abroad as often as he could spare the time. In fact it hadn't always been easy to take those weeks away from the business but he had felt it necessary to make the effort, since Edie seemed to get such a lift from these experiences. He had put that down to her childhood upbringing which, although not one of poverty, had certainly not been lavish. Edie had seemed to get so much pleasure from a few touches of luxury.

There had been many good times, and he recalled some of the highlights. There was the romantic weekend in Paris where she had loved trying out her quite good French, and going to the top of the Eiffel Tower, with its incredible views over the city. Then there had been a week in Madeira, with its dramatic cliffs, and botanical gardens, and they had both revelled in the experience of taking tea on the verandah at Reid's Palace. They had been served by deferential waiters and waitresses, in beautifully starched black and white uniforms, who produced the most delicate of sandwiches, and wonderful warmed scones with cream and jam, and cakes – everything so quintessentially English except for the setting! In Crete the amazing Palace of Knossos, built over 4000 years ago, had fired Edie's imagination, but then a strange thing had happened. On the return journey the knowledgeable guide had regaled her coach load of tourists with the story of the successful kidnapping of Generalmajor Karl Kreipe, war time commander of the German occupying forces, by a group of daring British officers, immortalised in the book 'Ill Met By Moonlight' by W. Stanley Moss. Edie had suddenly gone quiet, and looked very uncomfortable. Fraser had never understood why, and had really forgotten about the incident until now, when these memories were flooding back. Perhaps the loveliest setting, and the one they had both enjoyed the most, had been Bermuda. The beaches, with their soft, powdery, pink sand had brought out the child in Edie, and she had run barefoot, laughing, delighting in the sand between her toes. There had been many happy times to remember and Fraser felt pangs of longing as he recalled these events.

He was almost there. Now that he had conceived the idea of his mother living with him he was pleased – a weight had been lifted from his shoulders. He parked the car outside her cottage and swiftly covered the short path up to her front door. Using his key to let himself in he called out, as he always did when he arrived: 'Hello Mother! It's me, Fraser – I'm here!' Usually he would hear her reply, 'Come in, dear!' but this time there was no response. She must have dozed off while she was waiting for him.

He pushed open the lounge door, gently so as not to frighten her. Marjorie was in the armchair, and her head had fallen forward. He went over to wake her, and kneeling down beside her chair, reached for her hand. Between his large, warm ones her small hand lay still. It was very, very cold.

Chapter 14

John parked the car outside Joanna's block of flats and then went upstairs to ring her doorbell. After some delay Joanna opened the door, looking rather dishevelled – as if she had just quickly thrown on a few clothes.

'Good morning, Joanna,' John greeted her. 'Your chariot awaits.'

'I expect you'd like to come in,' she said, and led him into the small lounge, where he moved a few magazines so that he could sit down.

'Here's the paperwork. Your father has organised insurance for you, and I've seen to the road tax, so the car is at your immediate disposal.'

'How kind. What have you got me? I suppose it's a boring old Ford Fiesta.'

'No. It's a reliable little Renault Clio. It's not quite three years old, low mileage, the bodywork is excellent, and the interior is unmarked. I have tried to do exactly as Fraser asked, and find you something that won't let you down, and be reasonably economical to run, if driven with care.'

'It sounds,' she said, 'as if you have carried out your commission to a T.'

'I did take some trouble to find the right thing. Fraser's had a tough time recently. I was glad to be able to do this for him.'

'I'm sure my father has every reason to be inordinately grateful to you.'

John looked up. Something in her tone troubled him, and he wasn't sure how to react.

'I thought you'd be thrilled,' he said. 'Not many young people get a nice car handed to them on a plate. Your father has been very good to you.'

'Has he been good to you?' she asked.

'I don't know what you mean. Of course he has. He has trusted me over the years, and he trusted me to get this car for you.'

'And you've justified his trust, I presume.'

'Well, we've worked together in partnership for over twenty years, and there have never been any problems between us. I admire your father's standards – both with regard to his work, and in his personal life. I've thought of him as a good friend over the years, and I hope he feels the same way.'

'That would be good,' replied Joanna. 'It makes everything so neat. Tell me, does Sadie know you are here?'

'Know I'm at your flat? Probably not, but she knew I was sorting out a car for you. Why do you ask?'

'I just wondered how much she knew of your affairs.'

'What on earth has it got to do with you? But since you ask, she knows most of what I do. We've always been a couple who shared things.'

'I wonder,' said Joanna, looking as if she was musing over a problem, 'whether my mother shared everything with my father.'

'They seemed to me to have a very good marriage. Your poor father was devastated by her death. I offered to cover everything at work for him, for a while, so that he could have some time to get over it, but he seems to want to be involved still. He said it helped to have something else to think about.'

'I think,' Joanna said quietly, 'that my mother was a bitch.'

John was visibly shocked. 'However can you say such a thing?

'Probably because I'm one too – it takes one to know one.'

Your mother was the sweetest …'

Joanna interrupted. 'Are you claiming to know her better than I did?'

'Of course not. But it pains me dreadfully to hear you speaking of your mother like that. Whatever would your father think? He would be so upset.'

'My father has blind spots – fortunately for some he cannot see what is going on under his nose.'

John was getting irritated. 'I can't understand why you're talking like this. Where's your gratitude for all your parents have done for you? Where's your respect?'

'Where's yours?' asked Joanna.

Now he was floundering, and quite out of his depth with the conversation. Feeling decidedly uncomfortable the only thing was to leave. As he moved towards the door he looked back, and said in exasperation, 'Oh, go to hell.'

'See you there,' she replied.

Chapter 15

The funeral had gone well, really, Margaret thought. Of course, Marjorie's death had come as an awful shock. However inevitable such an event may be – and at 93 years of age it was realistically on the cards before too long – it still knocked you sideways when it happened. And poor Fraser! Fancy going to the house and finding her stone cold like that! He had been distraught when he had phoned her. She wished she was the sort of person who knew what to say in these instances. However moved she felt in her heart her mouth seemed unable to express the sympathy she wanted to convey.

Her mother had been very different – warm and gracious – people loved her because she could make them feel good about themselves. Fraser, too, had that comfortableness that made people like him. Marjorie clearly adored her son, and Margaret had felt in his shadow all her life. She knew her mother loved her dearly as well, but somehow there was this deep-seated feeling of being an also-ran. Fraser had already established his place in their mother's heart by the time she, Margaret, had come on the scene. Fortunately there was Derek, who had been a good husband for many years. Perhaps he was not the most thrilling person out there, but he never found fault with her, and she could feel at ease with him.

They had decided to have the funeral at the local crematorium, and had arranged this with the undertakers. The trouble with making it to your eighties was that most of your peer group were no longer around. However, that kind neighbour Sally had come, along with one or two of the villagers who knew her quite well, and of course all the family members had been present, including more distant relatives that they did not see very often, and some of their friends, too. She had also noticed that strange, dark-haired woman who had been at Marion's party slip in at the back. The vicar had taken the service very well, even though he did not know Marjorie – he had managed to make her presence felt, using the information she and Fraser had supplied and endowing it with an enthusiasm which had, briefly, brought her to life. Fraser, with great effort, had managed to contain his emotion most of the time, but Margaret had noticed that Joanna was visibly distressed. That rather puzzled her. She did not think that Joanna had been particularly attached to her grandmother.

When the service was over she and Fraser had thanked the vicar, and had stood outside the door to greet people as they came out. The dark-haired woman passed by – was her name Angela? – shook their hands briefly, offered her condolences, and then disappeared. Seeing her there reminded Margaret that she was the person who had caused a commotion over an umbrella at Marion's party, and when it was over she had realised that Fraser was no longer anywhere to be seen. Oh well, she couldn't really blame him for going early. At least he had made the effort to come, even if he hadn't been able to enjoy it. He really was cut up about Edie's death.

Now there would be much to do, dealing with Marjorie's affairs. The cottage would have to be cleared of its contents and sold. At least the will was straightforward – all assets to be divided equally between the two children. Margaret felt a stab of regret. She wished she had been able to show her mother more affection. Did Marjorie know how she felt? Margaret hoped that her suggestions about the need to go into a care home had not upset her. Anyone could see it was the sensible thing to do, and if Fraser had not opposed it so strongly she would have arranged it a long time before this. It was ridiculous for Marjorie to be struggling there all by herself – dependent on neighbours to see to her daily needs. Oh well, now it wasn't necessary, so at least there wasn't that to worry about.

But she did worry about Fraser. It was hard to see him looking pale and unhappy. Personally Margaret could not understand what there was in Edie to make him so deeply attached to her. Yes, she had been a beautiful woman – no one could deny that. But was she a genuine person? Margaret had never felt close to her. Edie would make all the right noises, but her eyes seemed to be looking into the distance and Margaret always wondered what she was thinking about.

She must try and help Fraser. She didn't know if the party had been a success or not, but perhaps she shouldn't try and push him before he was ready. What could she do? She hoped Sarah and Joanna were offering some comfort. Sarah was always busy, but the twins were adorable. Margaret regretted that she and Derek had been unable to have children, but thought that perhaps that was just as well, as she doubted her ability to be a good mother. However she knew that small children, in their innocence, could often bring a little healing to a sad heart.

What about Joanna? She had been in a strange mood lately. Something about her disturbed Margaret. Perhaps the problem was that she had no settled way ahead, and hadn't made up her mind what to do. It must be hard to see her older sister happily busy with her family and her work commitments. A thought struck Margaret – was that part of the problem? That she envied her elder sister and felt inferior? There was a familiar ring to the situation, which elicited a sympathetic reaction in Margaret. Perhaps she should try and give some time to her younger niece.

In fact, she would do something about that right away. She picked up the telephone and dialled Joanna's number – but there was no answer. She wondered what Joanna was doing, and was just making a mental note to try again later when the answerphone message clicked in:

'Hi, you haven't reached Joanna because she's not here, and what's more she doesn't want to be contacted, so whoever you are, and especially if you're you-know-who, just sod off.'

Chapter 16

As they sat at the kitchen table having a cup of coffee before embarking on the task before them Fraser had asked:

'The problems with my daughters that I was discussing with you – do you think it's possible that the girls will ever come to their senses? I hate to think of them struggling on, continuing to make the same mistakes.'

It had not been easy to settle on option one, but now that he had, Fraser found he was beginning to want answers. 'Most people do, most of their lives,' replied Angela. 'People seem hell bent, at times, on their own destruction. But that doesn't mean it's impossible to change. Usually it takes some sort of trauma or crisis.'

'Like, in my case, losing my wife and my mother?'

'Yes,' she replied. 'It might be something like that – although not necessarily so drastic. It might be a crisis in their own mind, such as a big loss of confidence, for some reason, that forces them to seek help. Something triggers the desire to come through the dark patch. It's not impossible. After all, you sought help.'

Fraser felt pleased that she seemed to think he had made progress. 'Well, I think I've delayed the inevitable enough now, don't you? Shall we get on with it?'

'How do you want to do this? Would you prefer me to sit here quietly reading a book while you look at the documents?'

'Actually,' he replied, 'I think I'd prefer the opposite. I'd like to do the sitting quietly, while you go through things and tell me what you see. I'm not sure I can bear to look directly at the papers, seeing her handwriting, and all her personal things. Does that sound rather cowardly?'

'It sounds pretty sensible, if that's what will help. I've been thinking, perhaps before we do get down to it, would you tell me a bit about Edie? I know so little, I think it would be useful. What was she like?'

Fraser's face suddenly came alive. 'She was the most beautiful woman you could ever imagine, with her lovely golden hair, and slim figure, and always so beautifully dressed.'

Angela thought ruefully of her own rather dark looks and fuller figure, and suppressed a smile. She also wondered, since Edie was in her fifties, whether the golden hair might have owed something to the hairdresser's art, but thought it better not to ask.

Instead, she said with a smile, 'I am reminded of a passage in "Sense and Sensibility" where Marianne is trying to find out about Willoughby, the dashing young man who carried her in from the hillside when she had fallen. She asks her mother's cousin, Sir John, but all he can talk about is how Willoughby is a good shot and a great rider – attributes that scarcely broaden Marianne's knowledge of the man. From your description, I'm no nearer understanding Edie's character.'

'I don't seem to be very good at this. How would you

answer, if I asked you to tell me about your husband?'

'I could simply mention the physical characteristics and say that he was a tall, slim, black American.'

Fraser was silent. 'Does that shock you?' asked Angela.

'It's just a bit unexpected. Was it a good marriage?'

'Wonderful, because he was a really kind, and thoughtful man with a deep love of his fellow men and a passion to help the suffering by using his medical skills. And then there was his sense of humour, which I always found attractive. Professionally, he worked hard, and would go on battling to save a life long after others would have given up. When his own life was brutally terminated I didn't want to go on living.'

'Same here,' said Fraser, 'I know just how you feel where that's concerned. I hope you will tell me the whole story soon.'

'I promise, but now we must concentrate on Edie. Why don't you try and tell me something of her life history, in a nutshell? A sort of potted version. Do you think you could? I think it would be easier to make sense of what I see when I look at her things.'

'All right - let me think. She was born in 1939 of Dutch parents, in Rotterdam. Her father was in the Dutch Army. Her Dutch name was Edda, and the surname was Bakker. As you might know, on 14th May, in 1940, the Germans bombed the city, killing many soldiers and also civilians. Edie's father was one of the army's casualties. By the time the tide of the war was turning Edie's mother had contracted TB and as she feared she hadn't long to live she was worried about her daughter's future. I think there were no relatives who could help so she devised a courageous plan to get to England, where she believed Edie might have a better future.

'She managed to persuade Dr Barnado's organisation that Edie would very soon be entirely on her own and they agreed to take her into one of their homes. Her mother then went back to the Netherlands, where I think she died shortly afterwards. The name was changed to the anglicised form, Edie Baker, and she quickly picked up English, as young children do, speaking it like a native in no time. She got lucky a couple of years later because by the time she was eight years old she was adopted by Pat and Ernest, who already had a daughter, Beryl, and they wanted a sister for her, knowing they couldn't have any more of their own.

'They gave her a kindly, if unexciting, upbringing, and Edie forged a close relationship with Beryl, who's been a real sister to her. She was fond of her new adoptive parents, who took seriously their responsibility to enable her to live independently. They believed her best route would be to qualify in secretarial work, as jobs were usually available in that line. Poor Edie really did not want to do that, as she longed to get into the fashion trade, no matter in how humble a capacity initially – but her parents held out, so she found herself at Pitman's College for Shorthand and Typing. For good measure, to try and add a little sophistication, they also started her on a flower arranging course with Constance Spry. It soon became clear to Edie, however, that the method used there was to spear every single bloom with a piece of wire, and she thought that was hateful. She walked out and wouldn't go back! But she did finish her Pitman's course, and was able to get a job in London with an insurance firm.

'Before long she had made friends with some of the other girls, and three of them decided to go into digs on their own. They had a great time, partying whenever they could, and meeting lots of young men. Then one day I saw her on the top of a bus, and I managed to get her to agree to a date – and that was that. Neither of us looked back, and a year later we were married. Along came first Sarah, and then Joanna, and the rest, as they say, is history.'

'Were there ups and downs?'

'Oh goodness, yes – life, for Edie, consisted of ups and downs. Much of the time she was bright, happy, full of fun – even excited, you might say. But I must admit she did sometimes seem to go down to the depths of despair. I couldn't find out what was wrong – she wasn't able to explain, only said that she felt 'low'. Of course I worried about it a great deal to start with, but I learned that she would, given time, pick up and become bright and happy again – and when she did she would be sorry, and want to make it up to me – then we'd have a wonderful time. I think I also came round to realising that it wasn't actually anything to do with me that had caused her such anguish, and that made me feel able to wait patiently for it to pass.'

'What sort of things made her happiest of all?'

'She loved the social situation – perhaps being at a party – she had all the men flocking round her, and she could captivate them with her liveliness – she never seemed at a loss as to how to entertain others with sparkling conversation. She'd come back glowing, feeling, I think, a great success.'

'And what had the opposite effect?'

'That's harder to answer. I don't really know. But sometimes she'd seem completely dissatisfied with herself – complain that her hair looked dreadful, or she was getting fat – then nothing I said would make her feel better – it was almost as though she was bent on hating herself, and she'd end up getting mad with me for trying to make her feel better. I inevitably put my foot in it.'

'That's given me a very good picture,' said Angela thoughtfully. 'In fact, you've done better than you realise. Well, perhaps we should get to work now. Where do you suggest we begin?'

'She kept all her personal papers in the spare bedroom, in the bureau. I rather think it's locked. Follow me.'

They went upstairs, and came to a halt in front of the bureau. It was the upright kind, with a closing lid, and three layers of drawers underneath. The first were half width drawers, and under them two full width ones, and each had its own lock. Fraser tried them all, and none would open.

'I was pretty sure she kept it locked,' said Fraser, 'but I've no idea where the key is.'

'Let's think,' Angela replied. 'If you were her, and you wanted a secret place for the key, where would you put it?'

'I can't imagine wanting to lock anything away. Why would I do that? I shared everything with Edie.'

'I think you're going to have to accept that she functioned differently. It seems there were things she wanted to keep to herself. So what would she have done? Put it in a handbag, perhaps?'

'I let the Charity lady take all those with her clothes. They were so personal, I didn't want them around.'

'Oh dear – are we going to have to go rushing round to the Charity shop?'

'I don't think so, because I did say please check inside the bags, and I gave them a box for any items they came across. They found a few things – coins, receipts, and so on - and left them in the box – and there was no key among them.'

'Where else, then, do you think?'

'It would need to be somewhere that I wouldn't notice her putting it away, so obviously not anywhere in our bedroom. More likely, I suppose, to be in here as I rarely came here.'

Angela started looking round. She tried the bedside tables by the twin beds, but they were empty, apart from a box of tissues. Then her eyes lit on a small console table in the corner. It was rectangular, and had two small drawers in it, and several framed family pictures on top. The drawers contained a few pieces of costume jewellery and some early photos of the grandchildren – but that was all. Then she noticed that the top was hinged. She removed the pictures and lifted it up. The contents of the drawers were now on display. She was about to close it again when it occurred to her that the drawers were very shallow – the depth of the table would have allowed for deeper drawers. She pulled them right out, and saw underneath a secret compartment - a small, built-in box, with a sliding lid. She removed the lid – and inside was a key.

Fraser's heart began to beat faster. He took the key and inserted it into the lock on the lid of the bureau, turned it, and heard the click. One by one he undid all the locks.

'This is it,' he said. 'Now it begins.' He sat down on the chair in the corner and put his head into his hands.

'I have to ask,' Angela said. 'Are you sure you want me to do this?'

'Yes,' he groaned. 'It must be done. Please go ahead.'

Angela drew up a chair and sat down. First she did a quick look through, and saw that the compartments at the top were neatly filled with various stationery items. The top drawer on the left had financial papers, the one on the right seemed to contain official documents, the middle drawer had photographs and some personal letters, and the bottom drawer contained travel brochures, and some other papers. She remarked on all this to Fraser, and then started at the top.

There were notelets, birthday cards, pads of writing paper, envelopes of different sizes, pens and pencils, and an address book. In the corner compartment there were some small cards, the front of which had pink hearts all over them. She opened the address book and flipped over the filled pages. This was not the time to tell Fraser that she had made a study of graphology – interpreting character from handwriting – but as soon as she opened the book and saw the marked backward slant of the writing she knew it belonged to someone with a strong tie to the past. The long, wide loops of the lower zone also revealed a writer with an emotional nature. She began to comment out loud on what she was seeing, and asked, 'Did Edie ever use a computer?'

'No, she liked to handwrite everything, especially in the later years. When we were first married she had a small, portable Olivetti typewriter, which lasted for a long time. But when it eventually gave up, she decided she preferred to handwrite. She never was one for modern technology, and computers frightened her. It's different for modern generations who grow up with them, and they're second nature – we older folk who haven't had any training can find them difficult.'

'That's very true – fortunately I did learn to use them, and find them a great asset, but lots of older people haven't done so. I must say it's all very neatly arranged. I'll start on the first drawer, the financial one.'

This contained bank statements, and old cheque books. Angela found the latest one, half used. She did not feel comfortable about looking into these, and asked Fraser if he wished to have them.

'No, it's as we said at the beginning, I want to use you as an objective observer who has no interest personally. You have my full permission to look into things and tell me what you see. She had a Savings Account, which I set up for her, and over the past twenty years or more I've paid in sums of money, whenever I had some spare. She was, of course, free to use it whenever she chose – she could transfer money from there to her Current Account, and she certainly didn't have to ask permission. But I did ask her to think of it as a sort of insurance for old age, in case I suddenly dropped down dead. That's rather ironical, isn't it? So without knowing anything precisely, I would think there should be somewhere between £100,000 and £150,000 in her Savings Account.'

'There's a statement here, with the latest balance, which is given as £15,565.56.'

'That must be the Current Account – and it shouldn't have all that money in it, really.' 'No, it's the Savings Account – it says so at the top. I'll find the Current Account documents.' She delved further and came up with another set of statements. 'That has £7,689.49 in it.'

'I don't understand,' said Fraser. 'Where's all that money gone? What do the details say?'

'The Savings Account simply says that amounts have been transferred to the Current Account. The statements do not go back very far, but she seems to have been transferring money for a while. The Current Account shows some amounts taken out as cash, and a great many cheques drawn on the account. I'll see if the cheque book stubs are here.'

She searched further, and found a brown envelope at the bottom of the drawer. Inside there were notes – a lot of them, totalling over £2,000. She saw the cheque book, and opened it. The stubs were filled in with amounts, but there were no payees' names written in. An amount of £500 was paid out regularly on the first of each month, and this had been going on for the life of that cheque book. She couldn't find any other old ones. She passed this information on.

Fraser thought for a bit. 'The cash could have been for the car which Joanna claims her mother had promised to buy her. I don't know why she would do that, but it shows her kindness – and certainly doesn't justify Joanna's outburst against her. Joanna also said that her mother had been giving her money. I wonder if those payments of £500 are what she meant. And what possible reason could there be for Edie to do that?'

'Can you remember Joanna's exact words when she talked about it?'

'Well, she simply said that she'd been receiving money from her mother – I can't think of anything else she said – and at that point I got mad and spoke loudly – I was asking her why on earth Edie would give her money – and that's when she told me to be quiet. She said "Hush."'

There was a pause – then they both said together, 'Hush money!'

'This gets worse,' said Fraser. 'I simply can't imagine why Edie should have to pay Joanna to keep quiet – whatever can she have had to hide? And how could Joanna possibly do that to her mother?'

'I'll look in the other drawers,' Angela said, feeling it was time they moved on. She looked in the drawer with official papers. She could see no sign of a will among the papers, but there were several certificates. Edie had taken classes at Adult Learning Centres, and had gained Certificates for completing courses on various subjects, mostly to do with Art, including one on Dutch artists, and there was also a cookery certificate. Surprisingly, one certificate showed she had taken a course on the history of the Second World War. In a separate brown envelope there was the marriage certificate, and in yet another brown envelope, which was carefully sealed, and was inside the first one, there was Edie's birth certificate. Angela frowned.

'What is it?' asked Fraser.

'I've just come across the birth certificate. You said Edie was originally Dutch?'

'Yes, born in Rotterdam.'

'Not according to this certificate. She was born in Berlin, her name was Edit, and the surname was Baecker. Her mother was Gertrude, and her father, Karl, was in the German military organisation.'

'That's not possible!' Fraser could not believe what he was hearing. 'She often mentioned her Dutch origins, and always showed interest in anything Dutch.'

'It seems,' said Angela slowly, 'that her mother thought it was better to use that story, and that was what she told the people at Dr Barnado's. After all, being German, just after the war, wouldn't exactly make you flavour of the month, and could well have put paid to the child's chances of adoption.'

'Then when would Edie have learned the truth?'

'How can we know, but she certainly did know it, because she has carefully concealed the facts. It begins to make sense of one side of her personality.'

'I think you'll have to explain.'

'If you think about it, Edie grew up with the knowledge that she had a guilty secret she must never divulge – a secret which, if people knew, would make her detestable in their eyes, simply because of the past horrors that Germany had inflicted during the war. Of course you could say that all this was the responsibility of the military commanders – one in particular – and that probably the majority of the German people were as innocent as the British civilians – but in people's minds, immediately after the war, all Germans were associated with what happened.

'Can you imagine what it does to a person to believe that if people knew the truth about them they would be hated? Edie grew up knowing this, and yet it wasn't her fault. Perhaps you can see why she was forever looking for approval, and trying to prove, both to herself and to others, what a great success she was – and how easily she could win approbation wherever she went. When her confidence was high she was as you have described her – happy, bright, sparkling. But if, for some reason, no matter how imaginary, she felt her stock to be low, or she thought she had failed in some way, she immediately believed she was disliked and her self esteem plummeted. She must have longed to be accepted for what she really was – but as she could never tell people the truth that could not be. So she spent her life looking for an approval which could never satisfy her as it was built on a false premise. Subconsciously she would have loathed herself, removing the need for other people to do so. Am I making sense?'

'I suppose so, and I wonder at my inability to see any of this for myself. But then I did not know of her German origin. You'd better go on.'

'Fraser we may uncover more difficult facts – are you

sure you can manage it today? Would you like to have a break from it?'

'No, I want to get it all over with. I think I have some idea now what we may find, and I've no desire to put it off and then have to come back to it another day.'

'Right. You're a brave man. Well, if you're sitting comfortably, I'll get on with it.' She opened the next drawer.

Chapter 17

'I must get on,' Sarah said to herself. 'I need to be finished here in less than an hour.' The children would be coming out of school and today it was her responsibility to pick them up. She knew all too well that she must not be behind schedule with that. But there were still a lot of loose ends to tie up in the office.

Trying to act as quickly as she could she sent four emails, put some brochures into envelopes and addressed them, and made three telephone calls. There was one more call to make but only five minutes left, and the number wasn't in her usual file, as it was a new client, and for some reason hadn't been added. She got flustered as she tried to think where it had gone, and started turning over memos and other notes in a panic. With three minutes to go she found it. She rang the number and waited. Eventually there was an answer, but Mrs Williams, the client she was trying to reach, was out. It was her son who had picked up the telephone, and he was clearly not too worried whether his mother got the message or not.

'Please,' Sarah begged, 'please write this down and make sure it gets passed on to your mother. I have made an appointment for her next week, on Monday, at 2 pm. If she will ring in I will give her all the details.'

'Okey dokey,' said the boy. 'Message received and understood. Over and out.'

Very funny, thought Sarah, who was in no mood for frivolity. Now she was three minutes late. She gathered up her coat and bags and ran to her car.

It would take twenty minutes to reach the school, providing there were no hold-ups. It was all within a 30 mph zone, and there were cameras, and plenty of warning signs. Sarah already had six points on her licence, and was anxious not to pick up any more. On the other hand, if she didn't push it, she would be late. Her speed crept up above the limit, and she hoped she would get away with it. Then her mobile phone rang. She did not intend to answer it while driving, but she did need to know who it was, in case it was an emergency. She scrabbled in her handbag with one hand, and fished the phone out. Then she waited until the traffic was fairly clear ahead, and glanced at the display. It was another client – who would have to wait. She put the phone down, raising her focus to the road ahead, and realised that she was bearing down on a pedestrian crossing, in the middle of which stood a mother, holding her child's hand, transfixed by the sight of this car hurtling towards them. Horrified, Sarah stamped on the brakes. The car screeched to a halt, two feet short of the crossing. The mother's face was white with fear. She shook her fist at Sarah and shouted something. Sarah dropped her head in shame. Her heart beat rapidly. How could she have been so careless? Suppose she had hit the child? She thought of her own children, and felt dreadful. She continued on her way, but now with extreme care, and arrived at the school, heart in mouth, five minutes late.

She ran in to fetch her children, and was the last parent to arrive. She mumbled apologies to the teacher, who said nothing – she didn't need to – her annoyed expression said it all.

In the car Kate said, 'We were the last. Mrs Wilson said she wondered where you were.'

'I'm sorry, Kate,' said Sarah. 'I got caught up in traffic.' The lie made her feel worse than ever.

'Can we go to the park playground on the way home?' asked George. 'Dominic says it's really, really good. His Mummy takes him there every single day after school.'

'I'm sorry, George. We do need to get home. There's a lot to do, and I have to get tea ready.'

'It's not fair!' said George, expressing his disappointment. 'Why can't I go? Dominic goes….'

'I know,' Sarah interrupted, 'every single day. Well perhaps his mother isn't trying to run a business. I've explained to you that none of us can have things exactly as we want. We need the money my business brings in to keep you both at that nice school.'

'It's not fair,' George mumbled, under his breath, knowing it wasn't worth his while to say it out loud.

'Really, George,' said Kate, 'you must learn to accept what Mummy says.'

'That'll do, Kate. I think I can deal with George without your intervention.'

'What's an "intervention"?' asked George.

'Oh, never, mind. Make sure you don't leave anything in the car. Remember what trouble we had trying to find your lunch box last week. Look, George – if Daddy gets home early we'll see if he can take you to the park.'

'Oh, great!' Perhaps all was not lost, after all. 'The

playground is really, really good – Dominic says so.'

But Daddy did not return early. In fact, he did not come back until the children had eaten, had their baths, and were tucked up in bed.

Sarah sat down to relax for the first time that day. It hadn't been too bad a day, in the end – she had got through all the main tasks she had set herself – and nothing untoward had actually happened, thank goodness, and now the children were settled for the night. Perhaps she'd use the last bit of time to finish the ironing, as Michael still wasn't back. Then she really would be on top of everything. Yes, overall, she was pleased with her day.

In the darkness of his bedroom upstairs George punched his pillow angrily with his fist, and then announced to his one-eyed teddy, 'It's not fair. Dominic goes to the playground every single day, and I can't go at all. It's not fair.'

From her corner of the bedroom Kate stirred. 'Be quiet, George,' she murmured. 'It's time you went to sleep.'

But George, deaf to his sister's instructions, was sobbing into his pillow.

Chapter 18

They walked along beside the river once again. Fraser had not said a word since they had left the house. Angela could feel him almost physically reeling from the shock he had received when that photo had come to light.

He had already found it painful to come to terms with the realisation that Edie had spent large sums of money from the Savings Account he had provided for her over the years, without so much as a word to him. He had always had such perfect trust in her, and now this was gone, puncturing the illusion he had cherished for over thirty years of his idyllic marriage. Then there had been the discovery of his wife's true origins, and he had been forced to acknowledge that, for whatever reason, Edie had been living a lie all her life, and had felt the need to reinforce it from time to time. But there had been worse to come.

The next drawer had contained an assortment of photographs. Angela had gone through these, and found both family photos and holiday pictures. The holiday photos had lead to deep and troubled waters.

There had been a few shots of Paris, and at first Fraser had brightened up, remembering the romantic break he and Edie had enjoyed there before the children were born – but then they saw one which included Edie – looking happy and relaxed – and much as she had done just before she died. It hurt Fraser to the core to think that she had recently gone there with someone else. There were views of other places Fraser could not identify – certainly not holiday destinations which he and Edie had visited. As a final thrust, there were photos taken on cruise liners. Edie had occasionally suggested, once the children were older, that they should try a cruise but Fraser was not keen. He wanted Edie to himself on holiday – and he knew his wife well enough to know how she would spend all her time socialising, and going to the dances. He had had no intention of sharing her with a boat load of people, so he had held out. Now it seemed she had got her way in the end, on several occasions.

All those trips she had professed to make to Beryl – to help with an ailing husband – Fraser had been forced to realise were fictitious. No wonder she had banned him from telephoning her there – on the grounds of not wanting to disturb Gordon. She had always said she would do the telephoning, and she had made a few calls while she was away, but not many.

Then they had come across that photo. There was Edie, captured on film one evening, when it was dark, dressed up and looking glamorous, smiling happily, the rails of a ship behind her. She was leaning back comfortably against a man. He had his arms round her, and was leaning forward, with his head turned to the side, so that his cheek rested on her head. She was nestling back against his chest. Because the man's head was turned down it had not been easy to see his facial features. But, for Fraser, there was something very familiar about his build, the way he stood, and his head.

'It's John!' Fraser had gasped. 'My business partner, John Stanton!' Suddenly into his mind there flashed that image of John standing awkwardly in front of him, wringing his hands in obvious distress just after Edie had died, and saying 'I'm so sorry. I don't know what else I can say – I'm so very, very sorry.' Fraser, misinterpreting the words as being intended to console him, had been puzzled at the time as to why John had been so emotional, but once he had seen that photo all had become clear. Other memories followed – John and Edie walking ahead down the road, turning to each other and laughing while he and Sadie silently brought up the rear. And Sadie, looking so sad, while John was 'away on business'. How clever John had been, Fraser had thought - he had somehow managed to carry out all his commitments to the business and still steal some times away with Edie.

At that point Angela had suggested they stop the investigations and go out for a walk. She had already seen the bottom drawer full of travel brochures, and had also noticed various bundles of letters tied up with different coloured ribbons. She had felt Fraser had already reached breaking point and didn't want him to have to endure any more pain. They had locked the bureau up, and gone out.

At last Fraser broke the silence. 'I feel such a fool,' he said bitterly. 'I must be a laughing stock. I've been going on about this wonderful wife of mine, and feeling sorry for other husbands because they didn't have a marriage like mine – and all the time I'm the one to be pitied!'

'You really had no inkling?' asked Angela.

'None whatsoever. Obviously I've been walking around with my eyes shut all these years, while my wife has been happily deceiving me. I was always ready to accept whatever she told me, and to humour her whenever possible – I suppose you'll say that's me taking the line of least resistance again. Well, yes, I did, and look where it's got me!'

'I think you never really understood what made Edie tick,' said Angela thoughtfully. 'And that was hardly surprising, as she took good care to make sure you didn't. I think if you can come round to understanding that she really was wrestling with a terrible feeling of disloyalty to all those who were kind to her, but especially to you, because of the way she rewrote history, and her various deceits, you might, perhaps, begin to see that she was in the grip of feelings she couldn't control. Her prime motive was not to hurt you - it was actually herself she was punishing, because she always had to live with the fear of disclosure. It was as if she was saying, 'As you will never find out the truth about my birth and parentage, I'll give you something else that will make you realise how bad I am – and then you'll really hate me!' And all the time she must have been experiencing a dreadful internal conflict – since on one level she certainly did *not* want you to know.'

'I suppose,' Fraser mumbled, 'I must have made things a hundred times worse by telling her how wonderful she was all the time, and refusing to listen when she tried to tell me about her defects. And she did try to do that – she tried very hard.'

'I think she was longing to be accepted and loved for what she really was – not as this perfect image you were bent on believing in. But then, we must remember, you had also been scarred as a small child, by a tragedy too big for you to be able to handle. And you had dealt with it by suppressing the bad news, refusing to refer to it, and trying to push the reality of it away. And this is what you have carried with you all your life. Edie wanted you to know that she was a blemished human being like everyone else, and that although she may have loved it up on your pedestal initially, the high position soon became uncomfortable and she longed to get off. She continually suffered from a gnawing sense of inadequacy that tormented her and gave her no peace.'

'But what was so terrible about being born a German? Alright, I can understand that immediately after the war it might have made life difficult for her, when it was all fresh in people's minds, but that's water under the bridge now. It wouldn't have made the slightest difference to how I felt about her.'

'Perhaps there was more to it than you will ever know. And you must remember that, as a child she had been indoctrinated into the vital necessity of claiming to be Dutch, that her true roots were a disgrace, and that she must never let them come to light. I don't know if you know, but whatever we are taught, or whatever messages we receive subconsciously in the first seven years of our life stay with us for ever. And when Edie became an adult, and perhaps had the ability to think logically for herself, well, I think she probably had her reasons for keeping quiet.'

'I can see, now,' admitted Fraser, that not everything was Edie's fault. She must have found me at times both stifling and intensely frustrating. I've never understood this before. Is that because I'm a mere man, or am I exceptionally thick?'

'Neither. You simply haven't been in a position to see it before. And I don't think you are to be blamed entirely for what happened any more than Edie is. You were both in the grip of these subconscious forces that neither of you understood.'

'You have a knack of putting difficult issues clearly. You've helped me to understand, and I'm grateful.'

'You've certainly had your fair share of epiphanies recently.'

'What are those? I don't think I speak your language!'

'Moments of enlightenment – when you suddenly see something that had eluded you before. A sort of 'Eureka' flash of inspiration. We need to remember that Edie's worst fears of discovery were, in fact, realised. We don't know exactly what happened, but it's clear that Joanna did find out. Edie must have been terrified that she would tell you. Your wife was a very complex character whom few could have understood, and many of her motives were subconscious, so that she would not have been able to understand herself what it was that drove her on this path of deceit and self-destruction.'

'I suppose you're right. Look, you've been so kind in spending all this time on me. I really think it's your turn now. I still don't know much about you, other than a few details I've picked up. I know you're very clever at understanding people, and knowing how to help them. You're the sort of person that others feel they can trust. You're also remarkably kind. But I would like to know something of your background, and in particular, if you can bear it, the tragedy you have recently been through. Could you tell me, do you think?'

'I think it's high time I did, as in all probability I shall be called back to New York any day now, and I think you have a right to know why.'

She began to outline her life history, running fairly quickly through her childhood upbringing, the problems with her brother, and his premature death. She spoke of the impact this had on her parents, and how her mother's depression had led to her decision that when she could she would like to go into the area of supporting people whose lives had been damaged by events and crises.

Then she told him about her meeting with Martin Makoni, during her mother's serious illness and death. She spoke of her admiration for him, how she had then come to love him, and of how good her marriage and her life in New York had been. She mentioned the counselling course she had taken, and her probationary work in the local community, followed by her job at the Mental Health Center. Then she came to the point where she had to recount the events of that fateful day.

Sparing herself nothing she painted a graphic picture of how she had heard the whole incident on her mobile phone, of trying to keep Martin talking while running to the park, finding him barely conscious and lying in a pool of blood, the race to the hospital in the ambulance, and the bitter news that it was too late – he had gone.

At this point she was fighting emotion and could continue no longer. As she broke down Fraser was moved by her sorrow, and gently laid his hand on her arm, trying to console her with words of sympathy.

Eventually she regained control. 'The tough part now is that I have to go back to be a witness in the Court Case. Two white youths have been arrested and charged with Martin's murder. I must go through all the facts in a Court of Law, and come face to face with the perpetrators who took my husband away from me, and deprived the community of a wonderful surgeon. I don't know how I'm going to manage it.' Again she wept.

Fraser asked gently, 'Could I come with you? Would

that help?'

'It's good of you to offer but I must do this on my own. I must keep focused on it without any distractions.'

'We'll be able to keep in touch, won't we?' asked Fraser anxiously.

'Yes. I think the best way would be by phone texts. Partly because of the time difference, and partly because I don't know when I'll be free, I think it would be better to keep to that. That way we can have daily contact.'

'Thank you. I would like that. When do you think you will have to go? I was going to ask you if you would consider coming with me to my mother's house. You know she kept saying she had some things she wanted to show me. Sadly she never did get around to it. You were such a marvellous help with Edie's stuff, it would be great to have your help again - but I know it's a lot to ask.'

'If it were just you, then of course I would. But there's your sister, Margaret. I don't think she'd be very pleased not to be asked. Perhaps you ought to do that one together.'

Fraser pulled a face.

'What's the matter?' asked Angela, smiling. 'Doesn't that prospect fill you with joy?'

'She'll probably boss me about horribly, but I know you're right. I need to speak to her about it. I'll do that very soon.'

'Anyway,' said Angela, 'I heard recently from the Prosecuting Attorneys, and there's a strong possibility that the wait will be over very soon. The trial is about to begin.'

Chapter 19

Heathrow airport was heaving with anxious travellers all intent on reaching their allocated check-in desk ahead of their fellow traveller. Trolleys collided and then veered off in opposite directions like dodgem cars. Faces scanned monitors for the information that would direct them to the right queue. Children wailed and mothers scrabbled through handbags for the vital documents without which no further progress could be made. Fraser wondered at the willing acceptance of so much stressful chaos in order to embark on a relaxing holiday. No doubt once each traveller had endured all the processes that must be completed and was actually sitting on an aeroplane with the promise of a little spot of paradise awaiting them at some distant idyllic location, it would all be worthwhile.

Angela seemed calm, walking beside him as he pushed her trolley bearing her large black suitcase. Her flight to New York was in three hours' time, and once he had lifted her case on to the weighing machine he moved away to park the trolley while she completed the formalities.

As they were walking to the departures point Angela said, 'Fraser, I have a confession to make.'

He looked at her in surprise, and said, 'Whatever can you have done?'

'Before I admit to my sin I want to ask you a question. Could Edie have had access to your mother's personal papers?'

'Oh, yes, quite easily. She would have seen where Mother kept them the last time she came with me on a visit. I remember now that while I was outside doing a few bits and pieces in the garden Mother apparently said she wanted to show Edie some photos. They went upstairs, and Edie told me afterwards she kept everything precious and personal in a couple of shoe boxes under the bed! It seems Mother had wanted her to see a picture of the father-in-law she had never known. My guess is she also wanted to show her some of me as a baby, and boast about what a beautiful baby I was!'

'And would it have possible for Edie to take something from those boxes without your mother knowing?'

'I imagine so. She could easily have gone upstairs while we were both in the lounge, on the pretext of using the bathroom, and removed something from the box without my mother having the slightest idea. Why do you ask?'

'When we were going through the bureau, or rather, when I was, and then telling you what I had seen, there was a letter at the bottom of the 'Official Documents' drawer which attracted my attention. It was addressed to your mother, and was written in September 1943. It came from the German Guard Headquarters in Warsaw, and stated that your father had tried to escape from the 'protection zone', and had therefore forfeited his life. It gave details, including the name of the SS Guard who was responsible for his death.'

'Really! That's very interesting, but where's the sin?'

'I made a quick decision, thinking that it would pain you to see these facts in their bald English, and I removed it without telling you. It seemed a good idea at the time, but now I don't think I can go away and embark on all I have to do without clearing my conscience.'

'You acted in what you believed to be my best interests, as you have done several times before, and I can only go on being deeply grateful. I see only thoughtfulness – certainly not something warranting the confessional. Nevertheless, I think I might like to have it, so that when I feel strong enough, I can read it.'

'That's the thing,' said Angela. 'I tore it up and disposed of it.'

'Then that's the end of the matter, and there's absolutely nothing more to be said. So please don't give it another thought. Go and focus completely on your own affairs. How are you feeling? You're looking quite at ease.'

'Don't be fooled by my outward appearance,' she replied. 'Inside is a seething cauldron. For a start, I am not particularly fond of flying, especially by myself. I could manage it alright when …' She stopped.

'I wish I could help. I really wish I could do something.'

'You are a kind man,' she replied, 'and you have helped me already. Thank you for bringing me to the airport, and for seeing me off. You do have a comforting presence. I believe you must have given Edie a lot of stability – my guess is that without you she would have been a very unhappy person.'

He smiled. 'Thanks. I must say you seem to know how to make me feel more comfortable in myself. Well, I shall be thinking of you – and I only wish you did not have to go through all this.'

'There it is – I must be brave. And I shall think of you also, as you still have some more discoveries to make before everything is done.'

'Whatever they prove to be, I think nothing can compare with what I have already found out.'

By now they had reached the point where the passenger controls began, and they must part.

'Well, goodbye,' she said, leaning forward to brush his cheek with a light kiss. 'Thanks, again, for bringing me here.' Impulsively he put both his arms round her and enveloped her in a bear hug. He felt her respond a little as she relaxed against him momentarily. Then she drew away.

'You will keep in touch, won't you?' His anxious, boyish look went straight to her heart.

'Of course. We will exchange texts, as we agreed.'

'Have a safe journey! Come back soon.'

She smiled, and then, turning once to wave, she was gone.

Chapter 20

'I don't know why Mother told you she had things she wanted to show you but she never said anything to me about it,' grumbled Margaret. She and Fraser were driving down to Marjorie's cottage, for what might well be the last time. It was soon to be put on the market, and Fraser had arranged for the contents to be cleared the following week. Today they were going to bring back any personal items they wished to keep.

'You know how old-fashioned Mother was,' replied Fraser. 'She probably thought the firstborn son should be the one to take charge of these things.'

'It's not that at all,' snapped Margaret. 'It's because you were her favourite. You always were, right from the start. I came into the world knowing the sun shone out of your eyes, and I could never compete. And in recent years it was painfully obvious. What was so unfair was that I did heaps more for her than you did. When I went to see her, which was frequently, I would tidy everything up, see to personal things for her like wash her hair, cut her toe nails, sort out her clothes for washing, go through any correspondence and see that bills were paid, and endless other things, for which she was not the slightest bit grateful. You just went and chatted to her, and she couldn't stop enthusing about your visits.'

'That's not strictly accurate,' replied Fraser gently. 'I did things, but they were more in the DIY line. I'd change fuses, and light bulbs, cut her tiny patch of grass, tend her garden, and so on. But yes, I did talk to her quite a lot – she seemed to want that.'

'Sometimes she got quite cross with me when I was there – once she even told me to go away – did she ever tell you she'd done that to me?'

'She said you kept telling her what to do, and I think she was rebelling against that, as many old people do. They like to think they're independent when they're not at all.'

'So when did you get so philosophical?'

'Look, Margaret, you gave her very valuable help and support, and I'm sure she couldn't have gone on living alone without your help. She didn't realise it, I know, but she did have every reason to be grateful to you.'

'She really shouldn't have been still living there – she should have been in a care home for the past year. It wasn't really right expecting all that support just so that she could have her own way. It was selfish of her, because look what demands it made on us – particularly on me!'

'Margaret, she would have hated a care home – and you know it. How could we push her into something like that against her wishes? I had to oppose you – I couldn't bear the thought of it. In fact, after Edie died, I realised it would be possible to have her to live with me, and I was going to suggest it that day I drove down and found her …'

'How on earth would you have managed? You couldn't have done the personal things for her – and you're no housekeeper! I suppose you'd have continually been asking me to come and help!'

'You sound so bitter, Margaret. Didn't you love her? I don't know how you can accuse her of selfishness when she gave up everything to bring us up single-handedly. She had very little money, yet we never went without. She gave us the whole of her time and attention. I don't understand why you're speaking in this harsh way.'

'You've no idea, have you? Because you basked in the sunlight you don't know what it feels like to be always in the shadow – to be the also-ran.'

Fraser glanced at her and saw she was dabbing at her eyes. He was shocked by the vehemence of her feeling, and suddenly realised the burden she had carried through life.

'Let's stop for coffee,' he suggested, and spotting a small wayside café he drew in.

'This isn't a good idea,' Margaret sounded defensive. 'I think we should press on – we're going to have a lot to do.'

'I think it's rather important to talk,' insisted Fraser, 'and I don't want to be distracted by driving.' He led her to a table, and ordered coffee and pastries.

'I don't want anything to eat,' began Margaret. Then she thought better of it and went quiet.

'I wish,' said Fraser, 'I had realised before how you felt. I should have done, because it was plain for anyone with a little bit of sensitivity to see, but I've learned recently that I've been going round with my eyes shut all my life, oblivious to anyone else's needs and inner feelings, and failing to understand the cries for help which I should have picked up. Margaret, may I ask you something? Did you like Edie?'

'Not particularly. But she was your choice, and you

thought she was amazing, so I tried to accept her.'

'Why not? What was it that you didn't like?'

'Oh Fraser, how can I say without upsetting you? Why are you asking these questions?'

'It's important, because I've been learning things recently that I didn't know, or simply wouldn't face, before, and now I've had to face them. I know I wouldn't listen to a word of criticism of Edie before, but now I want to know.'

'What's come over you? I've never heard you talk like this. Are you sure you're not going to bite my head off if I say what I think?'

'I'll try not to.'

'Well, I thought she was a play actor. I felt that I never really knew her. Sometimes you'd talk to her and her eyes would be looking at you but without making any connection – you knew her mind was miles away. She seemed to be going through the motions – pretending to be an affectionate sister-in-law - when in all probability she hated my guts. So I generally kept my distance as much as possible. I don't think Mother liked her too much either, and that was, I'm sure, mutual. After all, she stopped going with you to visit Mother, didn't she?'

'Yes, I think there must have been some disagreement, but Edie always brushed that aside if I asked, and just made excuses not to come. If I mentioned Mother she always spoke about her warmly, as if she loved her very much too. Which is exactly what you were saying about play acting. That was very clever of you to pick that up. You see, Margaret – and I find this very difficult to say – Edie was acting up to the hilt. I've now been through her private papers, and I've found out, not only did she spend most of the Savings Account I set up for her, not only did she falsify her origins because she wasn't Dutch as we all thought – she was born in Berlin, of German parents – not only all that but …' His voice trailed off, and he put his head down. Then he looked up, straight at Margaret, and said, 'She had affairs. She slept with other men. She even went on cruises with them – and recently she went on a cruise with John Stanton!'

Margaret was speechless. Visibly shaken, she finally said, in an unusually gentle voice, 'Oh, you poor man! Oh Fraser, I'm so sorry.'

'You had to know,' said Fraser agitatedly, 'and I had to tell you. But one reason I've done so now is to show you that I've failed, miserably, throughout my life to see things as they really are. I've taken the line of least resistance, and seen only the good things I wanted to think were there, and refused to face what I didn't like. Now you've been honest enough to speak to me as you have, and tell me how you've really felt, I can see that's why you've always been rather brusque in your manner. You've felt inferior, in mother's eyes, and you covered how you felt by being a bit defensive, a bit hard. I'm glad I know that now. I'm glad I understand. Perhaps now you know what a mess I've made of my life you may see me in another light.'

'You seem different, Fraser. What's happened to you? I never felt able to speak to you before. I didn't know you'd gone through Edie's things. That must have been terribly tough. It was brave of you.'

'It's kind of you to say so but in fact I was an awful coward. I asked Angela to help me, and she did the looking through while I just sat there.'

'Angela? Who's that? Wait a minute – wasn't she that weird woman at Marion's party – the one who suddenly

145

created an awful commotion about a missing umbrella which she turned out not to have brought anyway? Now I come to think of it, when that was over I couldn't find you. You must have gone.'

'Yes, that's the one, and now I'll confess that that was a ploy to help me escape. I couldn't bear it any longer.'

'Oh, Fraser, now I feel awful for having made you go to the party. I do interfere, don't I?'

'Actually, I'm grateful, because although the last thing I wanted to do was make any new acquaintances, it's turned out that Angela was probably the only person who had the qualities to help me, just at that time. She understood that I needed to disappear and she hatched the plot! She also gave me her telephone number, in case I needed to talk to someone objective, who wasn't emotionally involved at all.'

'So have you been seeing her?'

'Not in the sense of 'dating', if that's what you're thinking. But she has been helping me. Something came up with Joanna – she started to behave rather oddly and said all sorts of dreadful things about her mother, and slated Sarah, too. I was disturbed by her and didn't know what to do. In the end I phoned Angela. It turned out that she had a little time that she wanted to have filled, because she's been through the tragedy of having her husband murdered, and she knew she'd have to go and be a witness when the trial started – which it has now. But before she went she helped me understand a lot – it seems she has some sort of psychotherapy qualification, or whatever it is.'

'I'm glad you mentioned Joanna – I thought there was something wrong with her at the funeral – she seemed surprisingly upset. I tried to telephone her and all I got was an astonishingly rude answerphone message.'

'I might as well tell you this, too. Joanna found out about her mother's affair – I don't know how - and started getting money from her – a bribe, you might say, to buy her silence. Poor Edie must have been pushed to the limits – having to pay her own daughter not to give her away to her husband!'

'Poor Edie! How can you say that? She's betrayed you! She behaved abominably.'

'Funny – those were Joanna's words. Well, I certainly didn't think that to start with – I was furious, and unbelievably hurt. But I understand, now, that it wasn't all her fault. There were things beyond her control, and also, I blocked and frustrated her every attempt to tell me her needs. I must bear much of the responsibility.'

'Fraser,' said Margaret, 'I'd no idea you've been through all that, and I feel sad that, as your sister, I've been no help to you at all. I know I've been scratchy, and that can hardly have encouraged you to come to me. I wish you'd felt I could have been some comfort. But I'd like to say now that I am lucky to have you as a brother.'

'Oh Margaret – if only I had understood things earlier. Perhaps I could have helped you to see how valued you were by Mother. It's probably inevitable that the daughter is going to be treated differently to the son, especially when she's younger. And I'm sure Mother saw me in a kind of husband-substitute light – not very healthy for either of us, but in the circumstances probably inevitable.'

'Well,' said Margaret, reverting to a business-like manner, 'we ought to press on, I think. We've lots to do.' Then she softened. 'The pastries were really very nice,' she added with a smile.

Chapter 21

They stood outside, hesitating, reluctant to enter, looking at the little cottage which smiled its usual welcome, in apparent denial of the transformation within. Once they had plucked up courage to turn the key and open the door, the cold chill that met them announced the departure of its soul. No cheery voice called 'Is that you?' No fire glowed. Only darkness and gloom spoke of a vacant house that was no longer a home.

Neither of them wanted to break the silence. Then Fraser said, 'Are you all right?'

Margaret nodded. 'Let's get on with it,' she said, moving briskly ahead of him into the lounge. 'Where shall we start?'

'In here, I suppose.' They looked round the room and gathered up the personal treasures on display - framed photographs, one or two ornaments, the brass candlesticks Marjorie had always loved, and a wooden sewing box that somehow seemed very much a part of her. They stowed the things in one of the suitcases they had brought. Then they went upstairs.

As expected there were shoe boxes under the bed.

Fraser pulled them out, and opened them. At the top of the first one there were some lists Marjorie had made in a round handwriting that had recently become rather shaky. One list was headed *'Tell Margaret'*, and a list of items appeared below.

'say about the Care Home, say that I know she is thinking about my own good. She thinks I will be properly looked after. Tell her I will think about it, and meanwhile try and tell her how much I appreciate all she does for me. I know I wouldn't have been able to stay here all this time if she didn't come and do things for me so regularly, so I know I am very lucky to have such a thoughtful daughter. I can't seem to say it when she's busying about.

'say I'm worried about Fraser - he's so miserable without Edie - and ask her to try and keep an eye on him. She is very good at that.

'say I don't know what I'd have done without her all these years – does she know what a beloved daughter she is?

'say could she please not put my glasses in the black case because I can't open that one very easily – please use the cloth case.

'say where is my library book – it must be overdue.'

A second sheet was headed *'Tell Fraser'*. This read:

'show him the early photos of his father and see how happy he was and how much he loved his little son, and then how thrilled when his little baby daughter arrived.

'Try and explain that he left us so painfully – it hurt dreadfully – but he also had this strong feeling for his fellowmen back in Poland who were having a bad, bad time, and he wanted to help.

'show him the letters Allan wrote to let me know what he was going through and how much he missed us all. Say he and

Margaret have my permission to read the letters.

'show him the letter from the German Guard in Warsaw so he knows how his father died. This is important although it will hurt badly. Then ask him to tell Margaret everything – he has such a gentle way of putting things perhaps she will bear it better that way.'

He looked up to see an unusual sight – Margaret, always so controlled, perhaps even cold some might say – was struggling with emotion.

'I didn't give her a chance! She wanted to tell me things and I was always so officious I never gave her a chance!'

They began to look through the photos which were in another shoe box – small, black and white prints, taken on a Box Brownie, faded and worn with age, but still revealing a handsome young man with dark, curly hair, smiling broadly as he cradled his babies, and later, two small children together. There were also some with Marjorie and the children. The only ones that had Marjorie and Allan together were the wedding photos, and these, larger and of a better quality, revealed an intensely happy couple, Allan in his smart black suit and stiff, winged collar, Marjorie in her lacy dress and veil, both smiling shyly at the camera.

'What a short time of happiness they had.' The sadness of it was coming home to Margaret. 'What a pity mother didn't show us these before.'

'I think she tried to, a long, long time ago – you were probably too young to remember – and I wouldn't look, because I wouldn't accept that father wasn't coming back. I'm afraid it's my fault.'

'Where's the letter she mentioned, the one from the German Guard?'

'That won't be here,' said Fraser. 'Edie must have taken

it, the last time she came here, because it was in her locked bureau. Angela found it – I'm not quite sure why Edie felt the need to go off with it and hide it under her own papers. Perhaps, because she was German, she somehow felt responsible.'

'What did it say?'

'I don't know – Angela saw it and thought it would give me more pain, so she took it away. Then she felt bad about having done so secretively so she told me about it – but by then she had disposed of the letter, so I never will see it.'

'What a strange thing to do.' The action puzzled Margaret. 'I did think she was a bit weird when I saw her.'

'I suppose she had her reasons.' Fraser spoke defensively.

Margaret changed the subject. 'Should we have a look at those letters?' They both felt uneasy about it, but Marjorie had encouraged them to do so. Reading the flowing handwriting they were both overwhelmed at the depth of love tenderly expressed, but also by the horrors Allan described – the overcrowding, the disease, and starvation.

'What bitter-sweet emotions mother must have experienced when she read these,' said Margaret. 'So - he was in the Warsaw Ghetto. That means ...'

'That means,' said Fraser, 'he was a Jew. I wonder if mother knew when she first married him?'

'Of course she did,' said Margaret, 'on her wedding night!'

'Oh yes, I see what you mean. So, does that mean that you and I are Jews also?'

'I don't think so, because - isn't there this matrilineal descent thing? I believe that the mother has to be Jewish for the descent to be passed on.'

'Yes, I think you're right. So, it seems father died in the

Warsaw Ghetto Uprising.'

'You're the historian – my knowledge is dreadfully vague. Can you fill me in on the background?'

'I'll tell you what I know, which isn't an awful lot. I think that before the war there were a lot of Jews living in Warsaw, and they always congregated in a particular area together, which became known as the Jewish Quarter. But then the Nazis invaded Poland, and, well, you don't need me to tell you what their attitude was to the Jews. Soon they built walls around the area and closed it off from the outside world, and then began deporting thousands of the Jewish population. They thought they were going to labour camps, but actually it was to the death chambers. Those who were left in the Ghetto found out what was happening to those who had been put on the trains, and knew they're fate would be the same, so they decided to try an act of rebellion – I believe this was in 1943. They managed to build some underground bunkers. Then when the Nazis came for the remaining Jews they were taken by surprise to be greeted with fighting and they had to withdraw. Of course it was only a brief respite - it was like a gnat against an elephant – they had no chance really, and they knew it – their weapons were nothing compared to those of the Nazis. So then the Nazis set fire to the buildings and smoked them out of the bunkers with tear gas. I think most of them were either killed or captured. I believe a few did escape.'

'So what actually happened to father? Do we know?'

Fraser had another look in the shoe box. 'Look,' he said, 'Mother's made a few notes. My guess is this is quite early on, because her writing's quite good here. She probably did it from the letters, and from the news that was available.'

The paper was headed: '*My husband – Ahron Cukierman*

(name changed to Allan Coleman) Came with his family to live in England – life difficult for a Jewish family in Poland. Must have arrived about 1929, when he was 16. Father set up a Grocery shop – Coleman and Son – Allan worked there too. Parents died 8 years later – Allan changed shop's name to Allan's Arcade, went on living in cottage parents had bought.

I met him in 1937, married soon after – first Fraser, then Margaret. Allan was a wonderful husband and father.

He found out dreadful time Jews in Poland having – decided he had to go and try and help – torment over leaving his family, terrible, terrible. Within very short time Hitler overran Poland, Allan got caught in walled off area – the Ghetto. Soon after letters stopped. But I know he survived until 1943 – not one of the ones deported – still some left – they tried to fight the Nazis – no good – Nazis much too powerful. Allan tried to escape, but was shot. I have the letter telling me the details. With the name of the officer who shot him.'

They were both quiet, digesting the information.

'I knew father was brave,' said Fraser, at last, 'but he was even more of a hero than I thought. What painful sacrifices he made!'

'I suppose so.' Margaret looked thoughtful. 'But I suppose in some ways you could say how selfishly he behaved.'

'What!' Fraser couldn't believe what he was hearing. 'How can you say that? Father was self-sacrificing, surely, not selfish.'

'He went off and left mother, and us, knowing there was a strong possibility he wouldn't come back – and what for? What good was one man where the might of the Nazi machine was concerned? How could he possibly think he would actually be able to achieve anything? All he did was condemn mother to a life of loneliness, and financial hardship, and us to a fatherless upbringing. I wish he had not gone – then everything would have been different, and we'd have been a proper family.' And to Fraser's astonishment she began to cry.

'How can you feel it so keenly now, all these years later? I don't understand.'

'Because,' she sobbed, 'I feel as if I never had anyone. You always had mother's time and attention, and it made me feel so alone. Mother seemed happy in your company, never in mine. I was always the unattractive one, the one no one took much notice of. I could fend for myself. Fraser, the poor little boy without a father, was the one who got all the sympathy.'

'I'm sure that wasn't so.' Fraser was anxious to try and comfort her. 'In any case, you have Derek now, and have had for many years. How can you say you never had anyone?'

'Oh, I know there's Derek, and he's a good man – but I mean – oh what do I mean? I seem to have never been part of a family circle. I felt an outsider with you and Mother, and later when you married. Edie wasn't the sort you could get close to, and you were so besotted with her that the only things that mattered were what she wanted – I never came into the reckoning. As you know, Derek couldn't have children, which I was disappointed about, but accepted. I thought perhaps I could be a 'favourite Aunt' to your children, but that didn't work - they have no time for me. Sarah's so busy – I have my uses as a babysitter occasionally, but that's all, and Joanna won't speak to me. All these years I've wanted an older brother who looked out for me – I suppose you could say in place of the father I never knew – but you only ever seemed superficially interested – I could never really talk to you.'

Fraser was taken aback. 'I had no idea how you felt,' he said. 'I didn't think you wanted me around – you always seemed so prickly.'

'I knew you'd blame me! It's always my fault. Couldn't you see past that? I know people think I'm sharp and organising – but I have to be like that – I suppose it's my defence, in case I get hurt again. If people feel they can't get near me, then they won't try. I've managed all these years, and believed I'd got over it all, but now all these letters and photos seem to have opened the wounds I thought I'd got safely sealed up.'

'Margaret – I'm so sorry. I'm not blaming you - I'm blaming myself. Once again I've been so blind, and so involved with all that was happening around me I haven't recognised a cry for help when it's right in my ear. There's me thinking you were perfectly self-sufficient and didn't need me, and there's you thinking I wasn't interested in your well-being! What a shame it has taken Mother's death to bring us both to our senses and understand each other, the way we should have done all these years. I can only say I hope it's not too late.'

'I'm sorry, Fraser – I can see I probably send out the wrong signals. I suppose I've bottled it up all these years and you couldn't really have known. It's taken me by surprise, the way it's all come out now. I didn't intend to say all that.'

'I'm glad you did and I would very much like things to be different. Mother said she knew she was lucky to have a wonderful daughter like you, and I have always valued you as a sister, but I really thought you didn't want much contact with me, and for my part I have been very bad at showing you that you are important to me. I know I concentrated too much on Edie, to the detriment of all the other members of my family. What a tragedy that I'm turned sixty and you're not far short of it – and we've only just discovered we can actually talk to each other!'

'Fraser - look on the back of the list mother wrote for you,' said Margaret, suddenly changing the subject. 'There's another item.' Fraser turned the paper over, and read out loud:

'I must say something about Edie. I still don't know what to say. Sadie was so angry and so distressed. And if Joanna knows that makes it worse. I don't know how to put it. Perhaps I should just show him Edie's letter. I don't know how I will bear his pain when he has to read it. I must do this. I couldn't do it last week, he was being so kind, and he already hurts so much. But I must. Perhaps I should just give him the letter to read. Oh dear, I don't know what to do.'

'So, she knew!' Fraser was shocked, and wondered how long she had known. At the bottom of the box containing letters he saw an envelope addressed to his mother, in that familiar writing. In an agonised tone he said, 'I suppose I'd better read it.'

Margaret swallowed. 'I'll go and look through the rest of her things,' she said, pausing to rest her hand briefly on his shoulder before she left the room.

Mechanically, his face expressionless, Fraser took out the pages. The sight of the handwritten sheets brought images of Edie rushing into his mind. He opened up the pages and began to read.

Chapter 22

Dear Mother-in-Law

Thank you for your letter which came as something of a surprise. As you say, you broke the rule of a lifetime, and because you have never addressed me in such a personal way before, I must admit it was rather a shock.

I'm not sure that in writing as you did I would have said you were 'interfering'. I found the whole tone of your letter to be rather one of reprimand, or reproach - and perhaps you were justified in taking that line. At any rate, you obviously felt that you needed to say those things, and I admire your courage in doing so.

Your motive, I am sure, was to protect Fraser – something you have always tried hard to do. It must have been difficult for you, when he was only five, to have had to tell him that his father had been killed in the war. Perhaps I can remind you that he was not the only one to suffer that fate. And at least he had a real mother to bring him up. I have no memory of my real father and only the dimmest one of my real mother. Pat

157

and Ernest who fostered me were a wonderfully loving couple, and their daughter, Beryl, was like a real older sister to me, so in many ways I was very lucky – but even so, it's not the same has having a parent who is really your own. At least Fraser had you, and in you he had a real ally.

You say the happiness of us both is of paramount importance to you – but I would have hoped for a greater degree of honesty from you. It is Fraser's happiness you are really concerned about, and you see me as a threat to that. And what came as a really unpleasant surprise is the realisation that you also hold me to blame for some of the problems our two girls are experiencing.

Don't all girls, as they develop, go through periods of uncertainty, and doubt themselves? Why should that be my fault? Those remarks really hurt, as I imagine you intended them to do. I did my best by my daughters, and I don't see how you can now lay their problems entirely at my feet. They had a father too!

You are a very strong woman, Marjorie, and I take my hat off to your spirit and the way you have sought to do all you could for both your children, although it doesn't take much insight to see that Fraser has the lion's share of your love and concern. I wonder, have you ever stopped to ask yourself why Margaret is a slightly caustic, rather bossy character who lacks any real circle of friends? Is it possible that your upbringing of the two children, and the obvious favouring of her older brother, had something to do with that? Fraser laughs about her idiosyncrasies – but frankly, I don't like her, and have always made a point of keeping out of her way as much as possible.

Well, it's Fraser who is really the subject of all this, and I stand accused of risking his happiness, by my 'selfish, *unprincipled behaviour'. Is Fraser unhappy? Has he ever complained to you? Have you ever heard him say one word against me? Does he not lavish praise on his beautiful, wonderful wife? Surely that's something of an achievement on my part – don't I get any credit for that?*

Let's get one thing straight. I admire the very fine qualities your son has, and I have enjoyed all the benefits that come from being married to an upright, wholesome, affectionate, thoughtful, generous …. I could go on … man. I loved him so much when we were first married, and (you may be surprised to know) I love him still. I cannot imagine life without him. He has given me so much over the years, and I will always be immensely grateful and deeply appreciative. But …

Yes, there is a but, and I doubt very much that it is one that you would be willing to recognise, because in your beloved son's character there is a flaw – yes – let me spell it out - your precious Fraser is not as perfect as you think – and, over the years, that flaw has made my life hell.

How did he react when you told him that his so much loved father would not be coming back? Did he cry himself to sleep night after night? Judging from what you have told me, and what I have pieced together from the evidence, after the initial shock, he got on with his life. In other words, he shut out the unpleasant fact, and turned away from it, almost as if it had never happened. You told me some time ago that you longed to tell him all the details you had subsequently learned – that there was so much you wanted him to know – but somehow, because he would not talk about anything to do with his father, you put off raising the topic, fearful of bringing all the pain to the surface.

Was that well done, mother-in-law? What problems did you lay up for later life, by denying him the chance to face unpleasant facts? What now, of the man?

If I try to tell him something I feel I have failed in, he won't hear of it. I have longed to tell him how unsure of myself I have felt at times, how scared I've been, but he simply responds by assuring me that I am a wonderful wife, the best any man could have, and that does not help me at all, when I know full well that in some areas, I most certainly am not.

When we were married he put me on a pedestal. I loved it at first – I felt like a queen on a throne. To be so worshipped and adored was a new and wholly welcome experience. But the atmosphere was rarefied up there – I could not breathe. I wanted to come down and join the real world. Fraser simply could not understand my needs. He thought all he had to do was keep telling me I was perfect, and I would be happy.

So I began to need the approval of someone who knew me for what I really was. I started looking, sub-consciously, for a man who would love me 'warts and all'. I behaved outrageously at parties, and amazingly Fraser seemed to enjoy watching me flirt with the men there. Occasionally I managed to find a way to go back with one of my conquests – dear Fraser is so gullible – he always swallowed the stories about a woman friend who was desperately unhappy and needed company for the night. But I couldn't manage that too often. And you may despise me for it, mother-in-law, but I always made it up to Fraser afterwards, and left him feeling a very happy man – so what was the harm?

But I wanted more – something drove me on to try and find a more regular liaison – only then would I know that I was really understood, and if I could succeed in keeping up the relationship this would be the ultimate proof I needed.

Why John? You say that I took a man out of a 'perfectly good marriage' and spoiled it for them and for us. May I *ask how you know it was this golden dream of a relationship that you describe? You've met Sadie – a more mousey, dreary woman it is impossible to imagine. Believe you me John's eyes were wandering my way long before I became this wicked 'temptress'. I used to try and get closer to John by suggesting outings as a foursome – I even managed to get a weekend away organised for us all. But poor Fraser had such a rotten time trying to be sociable with Sadie that it was hopeless. We laughed about it afterwards – he said she had absolutely nothing to say, and he couldn't find any way of lighting a spark of interest in her. She was probably too busy watching John and me happily laughing and joking together, and she usually looked utterly miserable, so I gave that up. It wasn't fair on Fraser.*

Perhaps Sadie isn't so dim after all. You say someone has 'brought to your attention' what has been going on – and John did say recently that he thought she was beginning to have an inkling. It would be just like her to go running to you telling tales. It doesn't take great intelligence to work that out and it would be a nice sort of revenge for her. I can just imagine her delight in passing on her thinly veiled hints to you.

Of course we did embark on an affair – it was so exciting trying to find ways of meeting, and then having several days together at a time. It was fairly easy for John because Sadie was used to him being away in order to install his beloved kitchens in homes up and down the country. I shamelessly used Beryl as my excuse and made Fraser promise not to ring there while I was away – I said I just wanted to help her with Gordon, who was now rather frail – and it would be disturbing to them if he rang, since Gordon has to sleep much of the time. This gave me the freedom I needed and John and I even managed a few cruises and lots of short breaks in some of the most romantic cities in Europe. It was perfect!

Then that scheming younger daughter of mine spotted us – in the back row of the local cinema, of all places! And thanks to my training she knew how to turn the situation to her maximum advantage – so I have had to pass sums of money to her to buy her silence. Imagine being blackmailed by your own daughter! Fraser was always so generous with money – he wanted me to have a nice little nest egg in case anything should happen, and he would be appalled if he knew I had spent most of it on my 'adventures', and now my own flesh and blood is bleeding me dry.

That brings me on to my two daughters, who, you say, are of 'some concern to you'. Yes, Sarah does rule over everything rather rigidly, and makes sure everyone else fits into her schedules. But that's necessary if she is to manage a business, and a family successfully – and I think she's done an amazing job. Her business is a triumph of planning and efficiency and as a result she is now making quite a lot of money. She has a good husband and two lovely children and all that is a credit to her.

As for Joanna, she is a tough cookie who perhaps hasn't quite hit the jackpot yet but she will. I know she has the brains to go to University but I don't think that's the right thing for her – men don't really like bright, academic women. Oh, they think they do at the start, and say how proud they are of their brilliant wives, but before long that very success becomes a threat and they start to resent it. Believe you me it is a recipe for disaster. I want Joanna to have a great marriage that will mean she can fully enjoy her life.

I have tried to teach my girls the things that matter in life and how to achieve them. When they seemed to be moving away up some pathway of their own I made sure they knew where I thought they were going wrong. They understand the need to impress people, to charm them into doing what they want, and to go for what will ultimately bring them happiness. I believe they have taken my lessons on board. When Joanna has found the right man my task will be complete.

Fraser has trusted me completely and I know he thought I was a good mother to our girls - and I am sure I was. I find it extremely impertinent of you to suggest otherwise.

This letter has turned out a great deal longer than I intended. I did think of not answering yours at all – perhaps I should simply have treated it with the contempt I thought it deserved.

However, I decided it was high time that you faced up to few home truths yourself. Perhaps you can now see that life with Fraser has been a continual, torturing conflict of, on the one hand, wanting to live up to his unrealistic image of me, but on the other, wanting him to know that I could not – and yet not wanting him to find this out.

However, I want you, Marjorie, to know that, despite everything, nothing alters the fact that in very many ways your son is the best – he is the kindest, gentlest and most unselfish of men – and is totally without guile. He does not deserve to have me as a wife, and I wish I could have done better but I have always loved him, and – however strange this may seem to you – I love him still. So there you have it.

Your undutiful daughter-in-law
Edie

Margaret came back into the bedroom and found Fraser sitting with his head in his hands, the pages of the letter in a scattered heap on the table. She sat down

163

quietly beside him, aware of the tension in his body and realising his pain. Very gently she put her arm round him, and felt his shoulders begin to heave. Then the emotions that had been imprisoned deep within him for many years suddenly broke through to the surface, and his anguish was uncontrollable. His whole body became convulsed by agonized, racking sobs. Margaret sat there, her arm round him, not saying a word.

Chapter 23

'Joanna, could you possibly help me out by having the twins for the day tomorrow? It's half term, and I had it all arranged – Maria was going to have them, but she's let me down – well, she can't help it, I know – she says she's ill with a terrible cold and sore throat – so obviously they can't go there. I need to find an alternative at short notice, and I'd be so grateful if you could do it, just this once.' Sarah was trying hard to keep any note of desperation from creeping into her voice.

'Sorry, Sarah – not possible, I'm afraid. I'm busy.'

'Busy! Surely whatever you're busy with can wait for a day, can't it? I mean, it's not as though you are working.'

'There is life outside work, you know, Sarah. And it so happens that whatever it is can't wait.'

'Oh, *please*, Joanna. Do think again. You know I very rarely ask you to help me, and I wouldn't now if I didn't have to, but I'm absolutely at my wit's end. It's too late now to ask any of the other Mums – they'll all be involved in their own complicated arrangements. I'd relied on Maria and I've only just heard what's happened to her. Michael says he's already booked up, so he can't help me, and I don't know where else to turn. Couldn't you try and re-arrange things? It's not a lot to ask, is it?'

'Why is it that married women who have a family and have chosen to work think their needs take precedence over those of single women, who are currently jobless? I've already told you my plans can't be altered, but you're still assuming that I can easily change them and will do so for your benefit.'

'I just thought that, maybe, after all the meals you've had at my house over the years, not to mention all the lifts home Michael has given you because you didn't want to go on the bus in the evening, that maybe, just maybe, you might like to do something for me? But I can see I was wrong. Obviously your mind doesn't work like that.'

'Oh, so now I owe you this favour! Your good deeds are put in the balance and heavily outweigh mine - on your scales, anyhow. Stop putting emotional pressures on me, Sarah. If I could have done it, I would have done so, without you having to plead your case. But I can't do it tomorrow, and that's the end of it.'

'I don't know how you can be so selfish. You know I'm trying my best to juggle the demands of family and business. I work so hard at keeping all the wheels running smoothly, and most of the time they do, but just this once, Joanna, through no fault of my own, the plans have gone pear-shaped, and, much as it pains me to say it, I do need you. Can you really live with your conscience if you ignore my cry for help?'

'You sound more like Mother every day. She was the expert in emotional blackmail. She'd be proud of you if she could hear you now.'

'I can't believe you just said that. I've never heard you

speak like this before. You're so hard, and so disloyal.'

'Look, Sarah. It was your choice to have a husband, and a family, and run a business at the same time – not mine – I wasn't consulted when you committed yourself up to the hilt – so it's you that must take the strain of any repercussions, not me, and whatever you say, you aren't going to make me feel guilty about it.'

'So that's it! You're jealous! I know you've always envied my life with Michael, and my children – and you've been singularly unsuccessful in finding anything like that for yourself – so that's why you won't help me. Well, let me tell you something, Joanna, for your own good – you've got an awful lot of growing up to do before some man of Michael's calibre would look at you! I know we're extremely busy, but Michael and I understand one another, and we value what we have. I pity you – you can't seem to find anyone like him.'

'Is that really how you see your marriage? Well, I've got news for you, my oh so clever, older sister – you're deluding yourself. If you think Michael's happy with the life he has now, then believe you me, you have another think coming.'

'I suppose you'll tell me next that you know him better than I do.'

'That's certainly a possibility. What I do know is that you rarely consider his feelings. You treat him like some kind of useful appendage, a piece in your imperial jigsaw, someone you can control and use to fill in the missing blanks for you. He's just there to provide the necessary 'male role' in your family model. When did you last see him as a living, breathing human being, with longings of his own that he dare not voice to you? When did you last think about his needs, give him some quality time, make him feel wanted for his own sake? You've reduced him to the role of fitting into and helping with your relentless schedules. When did you last have a really satisfying love-making session? I bet, when it comes to bed-time, you say grudgingly to him, 'You need to get it all over in ten minutes, Michael, as we must get some sleep – we've a busy day ahead of us all tomorrow.' What's the poor devil supposed to do when his ten minutes is up? Turn over and pretend he's not a hot-blooded male? You're not being fair to him. He's a deeply loving man who adores his children, but he's never allowed to relax and enjoy them. It would serve you right if he looked elsewhere for someone who really values him.'

'Have you finished, may I ask? I don't know how you have the effrontery to speak to me like that. You know nothing about our marriage, nothing about Michael, and I won't listen to any more of your nonsense.'

'I know a lot more than you think.'

'I haven't time for this. This was supposed to be a quick phone call to my sister to ask if she'd have my children for just one day. I should have known better than to think that you would help me out in a crisis. I've no more time to waste.'

'Sorry if you got rather more than you expected.'

'I got rather less than I expected, and now I must try and think of another solution. I don't know when you became so bitter, Joanna, but it's a pretty unattractive trait. It's no wonder you can't keep boyfriends. As Mother has said on more than one occasion, let me tell you, young lady, such talk will get you precisely nowhere.'

And with that Sarah slammed down the phone.

Chapter 24

The children bounced up and down excitedly on the train seat, torn between looking out of the window to watch the changing scenes rush past and the desire to chatter away to their grandfather.

'I'm going to Brighton!' sang Kate.

'I'm going on the pier!' echoed George. 'Grandpa, what's a pier?'

'Well, it's…' Fraser struggled with a concise definition that might be meaningful to a six-year old. How sad that the twins had never yet been taken to Brighton. Sarah and Michael, good parents though they were, had not succeeded in squeezing in a family day out down to the coast, so encumbered were they with their daily commitments.

Fraser was apprehensive at the thought of caring for the twins all day. When Sarah had asked him, he had wanted to refuse. It had been no problem when Edie was around – she knew exactly how to handle them, and he had simply carried out the role of chauffeur, bearer of bags, and willing supporter of whatever Edie thought they should do. Edie could cope with all the little upsets that inevitably occur with small children, so that tears soon dried up, cuts and grazes were efficiently dealt with, and all toilet needs supplied. All he had to do was enjoy their company, and he revelled in their childish innocence, and wide-eyed curiosity. He used to love it when they came to stay for the night – he'd watch Edie, able to communicate with them on their level, have fun with them and yet have them perfectly under control. She knew how to enter their world and share their enjoyment. And she was so sweet with them when she tucked them up in bed.

Now he was having them on his own which was, he felt, a very different kettle of fish and a responsibility he was frightened to take. But Sarah had been very persuasive.

'Come on Dad. You know they love your company. You wouldn't find it any trouble if you took them out for the day somewhere. I know, why don't you take them on a train? They rarely do that, and as you play trains with them they'd especially love to go on a real one with you. Then you'll find the time will just fly by. Honestly, they're old enough now to be sensible, and I'll stress that they must do exactly what you tell them. They'll love it – and so will you! Please say yes.'

Then Fraser had thought of the idea of taking them to Brighton. By the time they had got there, had some lunch, been to the pier, and perhaps walked on the beach, or promenade, it would be time to come back. They would get an enormous thrill from the train ride! And this would make his task of trying to keep them entertained very much easier. He began to warm to the idea. The early spring weather was bright, and crisp, and not too cold. He had agreed.

Now, as he looked at their sparkling eyes and eager faces, and heard their happy, excited voices, he found a healing balm spreading through him. All the discoveries of recent weeks had been hard to bear. The agony of his loss had been replaced by a bitter sense of betrayal. Above all, his astonishment at his own failure to realise what was going on had knocked his self confidence. What sort of a husband had he been that his wife needed to amuse herself outside the marriage? What sort of a man was he? Suddenly he did not know any more. He felt numb as blow after blow had rained down on him. One thing was certain - there was nothing more that could hurt him now.

He brought his mind to bear on the present problem.

'A pier,' he explained, 'is like a bridge, built from the sea shore over the sea – but it doesn't end up anywhere – it suddenly stops. You can walk on it, and you see the sea under you, and then you come to the end of it.'

'What happens when you get to the end?' asked George. 'Do you fall off, and go into the sea – splash! And then you drown!'

'Really, George,' said Kate. 'Don't be so silly! Of course you don't drown. Do you Grandpa?'

'I think,' said Fraser, attempting to get the conversation back on to more cheerful lines, 'we won't have any more talk of drowning. When you get to the end there's a rail where you stop, and look out over the sea, and then you turn round and come back. But there are all sorts of exciting things on the pier – lots of rides, and shops selling funny things, and food stalls …'

'Oh,' breathed George. 'Magic! I'm hungry Grandpa. Will we have something to eat soon? I'm really, really dying of starvation!'

'You seem determined to pass out by one means or another!' teased Fraser. 'If not by drowning, then by starvation! What we'll do is, when we get to the station, we'll walk down to the sea front, and then we'll go on the pier, and I think we'll find a nice café there, where we can have our lunch. Will that do?'

'Fish and chips?'

'Quite possibly, yes, fish and chips.'

'Magic!' George settled back in his seat, happiness radiating from his eyes.

'What would you like, Kate?'

'I'd like sausages and baked beans, please Grandpa.'

'I'm sure that can be arranged.'

Fraser smiled. It wasn't so hard, after all. He was finding them a delight, and he was enjoying the pleasure of sharing in their excitement. This was going better than he'd dared to hope.

They had walked down the hill from the station, the children each holding one of Fraser's hands, skipping and hopping up and down, chattering non-stop – and suddenly they saw the sea! Reduced for a brief moment to a state of most unusual silence they stared, drinking in the sight and then the excitement mounted to fever pitch. They wanted to run, but Fraser explained that he wasn't very good at that, and they must keep to the same pace, and on no account let go of his hand.

It occurred to Fraser that it was a new experience for the twins to have an adult's undivided attention for a whole day, and they were revelling in it. Happiness radiated out of every pore and their anticipatory excitement was infectious. Fraser found that he, too, was looking forward to the adventures the day would bring and realised that he had not had that feeling for weeks. Since Edie's death he had felt there was only pain ahead, and yet, because of all that had recently come to light, it was equally hurtful to look back, so that he now existed in a kind of limbo. He realised that he had clung far too long to the childish view that only good experiences lay ahead, ignoring the inescapable fact that all doughnuts had holes.

Which made for a happier life, he wondered – spending one's days anxiously fearing that harsh events lay waiting round every corner, or basking in eternal sunshine until one day a bolt from the blue shatters your world, inflicting a searing pain? Looking at the children, happily confident that the endless day which stretched ahead would contain pure, untainted pleasure he longed for their innocence to last and prayed that no dark shadows would cross their path.

They reached the promenade. George stood transfixed at the sight of the waves breaking over the pebbles.

'Grandpa! Can we run down to the sea? Oh please, Grandpa!' George seemed to have forgotten how hungry he was.

'Yes, please let us,' begged Kate.

Holding each hand tightly Fraser lead them down across the pebbles to the water's edge. Then he picked up a pebble and skimmed it over the water, the stone bouncing four times before it disappeared beneath the surface.

'That's magic! Let me do it!' George tried, but with a marked lack of success. 'How do you make it jump up and down on the water, Grandpa? Please show me!'

Fraser demonstrated to the excited boy how to hold the pebble and launch it into the water so that it skimmed the surface before sinking. The first ones George threw simply plopped and disappeared, but then suddenly he began to acquire the knack, and set to work, eagerly picking up pebble after pebble, with varying degrees of success.

Fraser decided it was time to move on.

'Look, children – there's the pier! See how it sticks right out over the sea! Come on, let's go and find our lunch.' But George was not to be deflected from the enjoyment of his newly acquired skill. Surprisingly, even the word 'lunch' failed to move him. He went on and on picking up pebbles and throwing them.

'Come on, George!' exhorted Kate, 'you need to stop now, or there won't be any pebbles left for other people to throw!'

George paid no heed. In her agitation Kate failed to notice an approaching wave, higher than its predecessors, breaking on the pebbles and rushing towards them. The water reached her before she realised and by the time she tried to step back it was too late.

'Oh Grandpa! My shoes are all wet! And my socks too!' She became distressed and began to cry.

'Let's take your socks off.' This was just the sort of mishap Fraser had been dreading. What could he do? He didn't have a towel. He removed the damp socks and tried to dab at the girl's feet with his handkerchief. Then he put the wet trainers back on.

'My shoes feel horrible! I need some other ones.' She wasn't going to be easily pacified.

'Come on!' Fraser decided to try the masterful approach. 'We'll go up on the pier. It'll be drier up there.'

Soon they were standing on the pier, with the swirling waters beneath them. It was quite crowded – obviously it had been the choice for half-term entertainment for many parents. Fraser held on to their hands tightly. Kate walked with rather pronounced steps, lifting each foot as if it was a great weight.

'I know!' said George, as they were passing a souvenir

shop with some beach shoes in a stand outside, 'you could get Kate some jellies!'

'Jellies? Whatever are they?' Fraser felt distinctly out of touch.

'Or crocs!' Kate suddenly brightened up. 'I could have some crocs! Oh please, Grandpa – everyone wears them!'

They went into the shop, where Kate delightedly tried on some ungainly plastic shoes which looked, Fraser thought, rather like boats. She chose a shocking pink version – a colour she obviously considered highly desirable. She came out, a little unsteady on her feet, but smiling. Fraser, relieved that equilibrium was restored, carried the sodden shoes and socks in a carrier bag. Looking round at other children Fraser had to admit that she was right – it seemed that everyone else did indeed wear crocs.

While the other two had been occupied with the purchase of the shoes George had busied himself trying on a policeman's helmet.

'I wish I could have that helmet,' he said. 'Kate's got new shoes – can't I have the helmet, Grandpa? It would keep my head warm!'

'First things first. Let's start with lunch.'

Fraser led them away from all the temptations the shop held and they went off to find the restaurant. It was a relief to discover that their chosen dishes were on the menu and both downed their platefuls with amazing speed. Kate remarked that Mummy said chips were not good for you, and you shouldn't have them very often, but this did not seem to deter either of them from enjoying their culinary delights to the full.

'Now can we go on the rides!' cried George. Fraser suddenly realised that he might have done this the wrong way round – with their stomachs full perhaps it wasn't the best moment to be jogged up and down. He suggested they have a walk round first, so they could decide which rides they would like. They were quite ready to comply, and gasped in amazement at the helter skelter, the 'wild river' flume, and the water mountain.

By now it seemed safe to let them enjoy rides appropriate for their age. They started on the merry-go-round, each choosing a horse and climbing astride it in a flash. As Fraser stood watching them going round, laughing and waving at him as each circuit brought them near, he suddenly thought of Angela, and how pleased she would be to see him looking relaxed and happy. He wondered what agonies she was currently suffering as she was forced to relive every moment of the fateful night that her husband had been killed, and wished he could have been some help to her. It had been good to receive her text messages, but the truncated words and strangulated sentences had done little to paint much of a picture of events. At least it was contact, and for that he was grateful. She had kept her promise and been in touch almost every day.

The rides over, Fraser thought it was time to wander through the gift shops. He told them they could each buy one thing, and that they should also choose a gift for Mummy and Daddy.

'The helmet!' cried George. 'I'm going to buy the helmet!' He tried it on, and then spotted a kiss-me-quick hat. Replacing the helmet with this latest piece of 'must have' headgear, he went to admire his reflection in the mirror. Kate's attention was attracted by the jewellery.

'Oh Grandpa, look! A diamond ring, just like Mummy's!' She held up her finger, exhibiting an ill-fitting 'gold' ring with a cumbersome glass stone that looked as if it would fall off at the earliest opportunity.

Everything in the shop caused great excitement, no matter how unsuitable. In the end George came away clutching a 'quill pen' which had surpassed everything else in his estimation. It consisted of a long white feather ending in a ball point, and he held it lovingly against him. Kate had stuck obdurately to her 'diamond' ring. After a great deal of debate, they eventually selected a lurid necklace for Sarah, and for Michael a stick of Brighton rock.

The wind was beginning to get up as they walked towards the exit. George held his pen aloft, pretending it was an aeroplane, and before he knew it a sudden gust of wind had wrenched it from his grasp and sent it flying over the edge of the pier.

Just as he was about to bemoan his fate George's attention was distracted by a number of children with kites. There was now a fair amount of wind, and the kites were flying well.

'Oh look, Grandpa! Kites! Oh Grandpa, can we have a kite? Oh, please, Grandpa!'

'Oh yes, please, Grandpa!' echoed Kate.

Fraser hesitated. He had already spent a good deal of money on them, which he did not grudge for one moment, but he wondered how good it was for them to have every whim satisfied.

'The thing is …' he began.

The kites did look attractive, and the children running along the promenade with them were obviously having fun - and the twins' eager faces went straight to his soft heart. Anyway, it would help George to forget the loss of the pen.

'All right,' he said, 'we can fly them as we make our way back to the station.'

'Oh, thank you, Grandpa. Thank you – you're the best Grandpa in the world!'

Any lingering doubts dispelled, Fraser led them to the shop selling kites.

George chose one with a smiley train's face painted on it, and Kate chose a pink one with a fairy.

Once they had learned to get the kites launched they were completely happy. Sometimes the kites suddenly dived straight down to the ground, but it was soon possible to get them airborne again. Fraser worried that it was getting more difficult to hold on to the children, and he had to break into a run to keep up with them. The wind grew stronger and the kites fairly sped through the air.

Suddenly a strong gust tugged at the kites and George's string slipped from his grasp. He pulled his other hand out of his Grandfather's and set off at a run to catch it.

'George! Stop. Don't run on. Let it go, George! George!'

Kate was also concerned. 'Don't run George!' she cried.

But the little boy paid no heed, so intent was he on recapturing his prized possession. He was running ahead, darting through the people, when the wind changed direction, and the kite turned inland.

'George!' cried Fraser, 'stop! Stop!' Then, to Fraser's watching horror, George turned direction also and ran off the pavement into the road in hot pursuit.

The next moment there was a screeching of brakes and a thud – the memory of which would stay with Fraser for the rest of his life.

There followed a kaleidoscope of images, a mixture of sounds and sights. Kate was screaming, people were crowding at the edge of the pavement, a young man got out of his car, looking very distressed, another car stopped and a young woman went over to the scene and bent down, and others joined to make a little circle round the small form lying on the road. Fraser, distraught, and desperate to go to the boy, did not want to leave Kate. A grey-haired lady appeared and said gently, 'I'll look after the little girl. Leave her with me.' And she took Kate to a seat, away from the edge of the road, put her arm round her, and talked quietly to her.

'Stay there, Kate,' said Fraser. 'I'll be right back.'

'Grandpa!' Kate's face was twisted with misery. 'Is George dead?'

'I'm sure he's not, Kate. Just try and be brave for me. I'll be back in a minute.'

Kate nodded, and allowed the grey-haired lady to comfort her.

Fraser crossed to the scene in the middle of the road, his heart thumping so loudly he thought it would burst. The young man had gone white, and his whole body was shaking. In strangled tones he said, 'Oh God! He ran out straight in front of me – there was nothing I could do. He just darted into the road. I'm so sorry. I'm so dreadfully sorry.'

The young woman stood up. 'Are you his Grandfather? I'm an off-duty ambulance driver, I was just passing and I saw it happen. I've called an ambulance – here they are now, and the police will be here any minute.'

Fraser saw that she had covered the little body with her jacket. He had to ask the question, but he couldn't bring himself to frame the words. Instead he said, 'Is he all right?'

'There's a pulse – but I'd say he is pretty badly hurt. I've made sure no one's moved him.'

Everyone stood back to let the paramedics through. They did their examination, and then turned to Fraser.

'We're taking him to the East Sussex County Hospital – they're ready to receive him. We need you to come in the Ambulance, Sir – there are some questions we shall have to ask.'

'What about Kate?' asked Fraser, in anguish. 'I don't know what to do about her. She's with that lady over there. I can't take her to the hospital – she'll be too frightened.'

The policeman intervened. 'We'll get a WPC to look after her, sir. We'll take her to the Police Station until her parents can fetch her. Don't worry, she'll be fine with us. Just go and tell her that's what's going to happen, and then you must get in the Ambulance. The boy needs to be rushed to the hospital.'

Fraser went to speak to Kate. 'Look Kate, George needs some treatment, and we have to get him to the hospital quickly. Now, I want you to be very brave, and let a nice police lady look after you, and take you to the Police Station, to wait for Mummy and Daddy. They'll come and take you back home. Will you do that for me Kate? It's what will help George most of all.'

With tears running down her face Kate solemnly nodded. She was holding on tightly to the grey-haired lady's hand. The lady promised she would stay with Kate until the woman police officer arrived. Fraser ran back to see that George was now on a stretcher, and the paramedics were gently lifting him into the ambulance. He turned to thank the young woman. She had written her name and address on a piece of paper. 'Just in case you want to contact me,' she said. 'I saw the whole thing happen.' Fraser tried to thank her but choked over his words. She smiled reassuringly, and he got into the ambulance.

The hospital staff swung into action. George, hooked up to tubes, was hurried into the theatre, and Fraser was shown into a small waiting room. The police officer arrived, sat down with him, and took out his notebook.

'What about the parents? Where are they?'

Fraser groaned. 'It's my daughter and son-in-law,' he said. 'I don't know how to tell them. They entrusted the twins to me for the day, and look what's happened! I've failed them miserably! I can't face telling them, but I must.'

'We could do that for you, sir, if you like. That might be better – we can give them details of exactly where the hospital is, and where Kate is. Would you like us to do that?'

'I suppose so. I don't know what to say. I feel so dreadful. I'll never forgive myself.'

'Look, sir, children do this sort of thing. No matter how often you tell them they still run into the road – I've seen it happen many times before. You mustn't blame yourself.'

'Oh but I do, and I must. I was responsible for George! I wonder how long it will be before there's any news?'

'I'm sure they'll tell you as soon as they can. Now, sir, I'm going to get them to bring you a strong cup of tea, and I'll make the phone calls. Just give me the names and telephone numbers.'

He went off, and a kind nurse appeared with the tea. Mechanically Fraser took it, and then put it down. The nurse encouraged him to drink it, saying it was good for shock.

That's it, thought Fraser. I've had a dreadful shock. I don't know how I'll ever get over it. My poor little Kate, poor Sarah and Michael. Oh my dear little George. He put his head into his hands and sat there, trying to endure the agonising pain.

The police officer came back. He told Fraser that he had spoken to the boy's mother.

'Was she dreadfully upset?' asked Fraser.

The officer hesitated. It would certainly be better not to report the mother's original hysterical reaction to this grandfather who, anyone could see, was desperately worried. 'She was obviously shaken,' he said, 'but she was able to think clearly about what she needed to do. She's going to try and contact her husband, so that they can come down together, but if she can't, she'll get her colleague to accompany her. She realises it would be preferable for her not to drive down by herself.'

Fraser nodded dumbly. The officer left him, and he settled down to wait for news. Suddenly he knew what he wanted to do. He went outside, and turning on his mobile phone, pressed Angela's number. To his astonishment, she responded.

'Fraser! Is everything all right?'

'No, I'm afraid it's not – it's terrible. Look, can you talk? Is this a good moment?'

'Actually it's a very good one – we've come out for a break, and I'd just turned on the phone to see if there were any messages. What's happened?'

Stumbling through the words, his voice breaking, Fraser conveyed briefly what had taken place.

Her deep, warm voice coming down the airwaves, brought an immense feeling of relief, even if only temporarily. 'Oh, you poor, poor man. I am so sorry. What you must be going through! Oh, Fraser.'

'The thing is,' he sobbed, 'unable to control his feelings

any more, 'it's all my fault. I didn't take good enough care of him. I had charge of him and I failed him and the family. I'll never be able to forgive myself.'

'Fraser, you did all you could. Children can run off, despite our best efforts. But the ultimate responsibility is Sarah's – she wanted to pass the children on to someone else. When did she ask you?'

'Yesterday.'

'My guess is you were a last resort. She wouldn't have left it to the last moment. Perhaps someone else pulled out. Look Fraser, Sarah and Michael were the parents, and neither of them would assume responsibility for their children. They passed it on, and if they chose someone who could not run to keep up with the children, then there are logical consequences to that.'

Fraser found he was breathing just a little more easily. 'I'm so sorry to have troubled you with this. I know I shouldn't have, when you have so much going on. How is everything?'

'It's drawing to a close now. Probably only another day, or perhaps two. I think there'll be a conviction. Anyhow, I'm so glad you rang, and just at this moment, too, when I could speak. I shall think of you, and young George. Stay brave, Fraser. We must believe. I'll believe if you will.'

'I'll try,' he promised. 'And thank you so much, Angela. Once again you've been my guardian angel! I don't think I could have managed without speaking to you.'

He went back inside, the seeds of a little more courage planted in his heart, and sat down to wait for news.

Chapter 25

At last the doctor stood before him. Fraser waited apprehensively.

'He's had a bit of a bump on the head,' said the doctor, sounding as if all that was needed was a piece of sticking plaster and George would be fine.

Fraser said, 'He's alive, thank God.'

'He's alive,' replied the doctor. Now we come to the serious bit, thought Fraser. 'But he's badly concussed. He hasn't come round yet, so we can't tell the extent of the damage. He's got some broken bones – ribs, femur – but those will heal, given time.'

What he's implying, thought Fraser, is that his brain may not. And there may not even be time for his bones to heal.

'So what now?' he asked. He wished doctors would say the things you really wanted to hear.

'We've dealt with the broken bones, and we're moving him to the intensive care unit, where he'll have 24-hour monitoring. It's a question of when he regains consciousness.'

Or if, thought Fraser. Oh, please God, when, rather than if.

'Can I see him?' he asked.

'Shortly, when the move has been completed.' The doctor hesitated. 'Just be aware that he's in a critical state, and you won't see much of him for tubes and other support mechanisms.'

Fraser nodded. 'I'd like to see him all the same, if I may. Thank you for everything you've done.'

He was instructed to go on waiting, and they would call him when they were ready.

A nurse brought him a sandwich. How kind everyone was. The last thing he felt like was eating, but the thoughtfulness touched him. The receptionist came to tell him that there had been a call from the police station, and they would like him to speak to Kate. The receptionist showed him where he could take the call.

'Grandpa!' said Kate. 'Is it my fault?'

'How can it be?' asked Fraser. 'I was the one who was supposed to be looking after the two of you, and I let him run off.'

'But all I did was call out to him!' Kate was very agitated. 'I tried to make him stop by shouting at him! I should have run after him and made him stop. It's all my fault! And now George is going to die, and it's my fault!'

He did his best reassure the little girl. He said she did the right thing by staying with him – it would only have made things worse if she had run off too. He tried to absolve her from the responsibility which she had assumed, and to reassure her about George. He told her George was not going to die, and was being given excellent treatment, and they must wait patiently. She wanted to come and see her brother but Fraser said it wasn't possible yet, because they were still attending to him. The WPC came on the line and said Kate was being very good, and very brave, but she was worrying that somehow she had been to blame, and they were all trying to keep her calm. She also reported that there had been calls from the mother to say when she would arrive – and it would probably be another half an hour, and she would go the hospital first. Apparently Sarah had not been able to get hold of Michael at the time, but she had since done so, and he was on his way down also.

When he had finished the call the receptionist asked him how he was. Fraser, who was still feeling numb, tried to think about it, and suddenly had the overwhelming conviction that he must not lose this physical closeness to George until the child did regain consciousness. He explained this to the receptionist and asked her if she knew of somewhere he could stay, near the hospital, for a night or two – or however long it took. She proved most helpful, and finding the name of a small hotel nearby, telephoned and spoke to the proprietor, who confirmed that a room was available. Fraser then spoke to this Mrs Stanbury explaining what the situation was, and she said Fraser could come at whatever time was convenient for him, and she offered her best wishes for his grandson's recovery. She said she might even be able to find him a spare pair of pyjamas and a toothbrush.

The next ordeal would be seeing Sarah, and Michael. He went back to the room that was becoming all too familiar. About half an hour later Sarah arrived.

'Oh, Sarah!' He held out his arms and she went to him. He clasped her close, and thought what a pity it was that it took this crisis for such an embrace to be possible. Normally a peremptory peck on the cheek was all he got.

'I'm so sorry, Sarah,' he said through tears. 'I'm so

desperately sorry. I've let you down in the worst possible way. I feel so dreadful.'

She pulled away from him. He was shocked by her white, tear-stained face, and the anguished emotions that he saw there.

'Don't say that, Dad. Don't say that. It's my fault. I should never have pushed you into doing it. I got let down by Maria, and Joanna refused to help, and I didn't know where else to turn. I've let my business life get so important I can't even take a day off for my children! Well, whatever happens, I'm going to make some changes. I seem to have lost sight of my priorities and I'm going to have a rethink – but you must not blame yourself. Is there any more news?'

At that moment a nurse came to tell them they could come with her and see George. Clutching Fraser's arm, Sarah struggled to control her emotions and together they followed the nurse, until they were standing by George's bedside. On the way the nurse had told them not to be alarmed by the array of machines and wires and tubes that were involved – these were all part of the monitoring process. It was a good thing she had warned them, because the sight of the apparatus was daunting, and George's head was so swathed in bandages that there was very little of him to be seen. His eyes were closed, he looked deathly pale, and the swelling under the blankets told of his plastered leg.

In a small voice Sarah whispered, 'I love you, George.'

They were allowed to stay for a short while, and then they went back downstairs. Fraser told Sarah of his plan to stay nearby, and she thought that was a wonderful idea.

'I must take Kate home. I've got to try and make life proceed as normally as possible for her. It would be so good to know that you were on the spot.'

A few minutes later Michael arrived. Fraser was pleased to see how the parents clung together, and felt that such solidarity would at least give them both some strength. Sarah went off to collect Kate – Lydia, her colleague, had been patiently sitting in the car all this time – and Michael went to see George. Fraser decided to wait until he returned before going off to find his accommodation.

When Michael came back he looked shaken. He sat down with Fraser, and for a while couldn't speak. Then he said, 'I want you to know that neither Sarah nor I blame you for what has happened. We blame ourselves, both of us. It was my fault as much as it was Sarah's. We should never have given you the responsibility. I'm sorry you've had to go through all this. You've recently lost your wife, and your mother – and now there's this crisis for you to bear. I know how fond you are of the little lad.'

'Thank you, Michael, for saying that. Of course, I do feel dreadfully responsible, I can't help it. We must just go on believing. That's what we have to do.'

Michael nodded. He seemed to want to say more, but didn't do so.

'Sarah and I will probably take turns to come down – I think it's important we don't leave Kate.'

'About Kate,' said Fraser. 'I think you should know that she feels responsible, too. She shouted to George to stop, but she thinks she should have run after him. You and Sarah will have to try and make sure she doesn't go on carrying that burden on her tiny shoulders.'

'Thank you for telling me,' said Michael. 'There's been too much emphasis on fault and who's to blame in our house. I'll make sure we talk to her about it.'

There's was nothing more he could do. Fraser decided

it was time to leave the hospital, and try and get some sleep. He would return early, and await any developments the next day.

Chapter 26

To Fraser's surprise the first person on the scene the next morning was Joanna. After a pleasant breakfast at The Poplars – which he had not been able to do justice to – Fraser had made his way straight to the hospital, where he reported to Reception. The girl contacted the Intensive Care unit for an update, and he learned there was no change in George's condition. He still lay in a coma. Fraser went to say 'Good morning' to George, and then sat in the small waiting room, where he had spent so much time the previous day. It was little more than 9.30 am when Joanna had arrived.

Not only was Fraser taken aback to see her there so early, but he was also astonished at her appearance. He face was white and strained, and her eyes puffy. She looked as it she had been awake all night.

'Joanna! What are you doing here so early?' Although the twins were fond of their Aunt, and she, for her part, took a mild interest in them, Fraser wouldn't have said there was a special relationship between them. Of course what had happened was dreadful, but he couldn't understand why she looked quite so shaken.

'I had to come,' she said. 'I've been out of my mind with worry. Is there any news?'

'No change,' said Fraser. 'That's what they told me this morning – I've been to see him.'

'Are you going to stay here all the time?'

'Yes,' he said – 'for as long as it takes.'

'Why on earth are you doing that? Surely it's for Sarah and Michael to arrange to be here all the time. Why should you do it?'

'Because I want to,' replied Fraser, 'and because I love the child. And also because I feel very much to blame.'

'You are not to blame!' Joanna's voice was rising. 'How can it be your fault when George is not your responsibility? You should never have been asked to look after the twins. It wasn't fair to ask you. Sarah should have been looking after them. They're her children!'

Her vehemence was disturbing. Fraser couldn't understand why her feelings were so strong.

'I gather Sarah had an important business appointment, and so did Michael. I believe Sarah asked you, as well, but you couldn't help either. I thought perhaps I could manage, if I took them out for the day, but it all went horribly wrong.'

'How can Sarah be too busy to look after her own children? Why on earth did she have them if she doesn't want to look after them?'

Joanna was trembling and her words were coming out in bursts. She seemed wretched.

'Steady on,' said Fraser. 'Lots of mothers work, and cope with bringing up children. Sarah's not alone. I suppose they feel they're doing the best they can for their families, by bringing in a good income. Anyway, if the wife is working the father must play a full role as well. Apparently Sarah couldn't get hold of Michael for some time, until … well, after it happened. I don't know where he was.'

'He was with me.'

'What? What on earth was he doing with you?'

'Having mad, bad, wonderful sex!' Joanna glared defiantly at her father. Startled, and uncomprehending, Fraser started to say, 'Whatever do you mean? Surely he …' but Joanna interrupted, and it all came out in a rush, like wine pouring from an uncorked bottle.

'Michael and I were having an affair. Only it didn't feel like an affair. It felt like healing for both body and soul, like finding an outlet for the frustrations of unfulfilled lives, like revenge – yes revenge – against a self-righteous, smug sister who thinks she's so marvellous at everything she does, and who hasn't the slightest idea what all her controlling schemes are doing to her family. That was my motivation – and Michael – poor love, he just wanted to be wanted, wanted because he is a man, wanted because he is who he is, wanted for everything he could bring to the marriage, and not feel side-lined into becoming a small cog in Sarah's constantly spinning wheel.'

Fraser was flabbergasted. The intensity of the emotions caught him by surprise, and coming, as they did, at a time when he was feeling raw with the pain of worry and fear for his grandson's life, he felt himself reeling under it, unable to grasp what he was hearing, unable to respond.

'Don't think I'm proud of myself,' continued Joanna in a low voice. 'I hate myself, for what I've done, for the way I've hurt people, for my own failure to make anything of myself, and for what I did to Mother. I … I wasn't very nice to her, and now it's too late.'

'I know what you did,' said Fraser, wearily. 'I found out everything. I know what she did, and what you did.'

'You know?' It was Joanna's turn to be amazed. 'You know, but you haven't said. You even bought me that car!'

'I didn't know then, but I do now. You see, Joanna, I know what it feels like when your partner deceives you. Sarah will have to be told, and she will have to suffer, as I have done.'

'Oh Dad!' Joanna looked shocked. She put out her hand to him. 'I didn't know you've been going through all that. I've been so taken up with my own grievances I've given little thought to you. I wish I'd been more help to you. I wish I hadn't taken what I'd no right to take. Michael and I found incredible solace with each other, and now that has to go.' She began to cry.

'Yes,' said Fraser, 'it must – and it wasn't really what you thought – it was only an illusion of solace. In the long run it was only going to lead to misery and heartbreak for everyone. And on top of that we must all endure the worry about our dear young George.'

'I don't think I can face him,' said Joanna. 'I can't bear to look, and think that he's like that because of me. I don't want to see him.'

'You must,' said Fraser. 'You must go and see him, and say hello to him as if he can hear you. And then you make him silent promises – commitments you are one hundred per cent sure you mean, and you will keep.'

Joanna nodded. She appeared to be gathering up her courage, and then she got up and walked towards the outer door to the unit.

Ten minutes later she returned. This time she looked a little calmer.

'I did what you said, and I sat by him, and I made my promises. Oh, the poor little chap – he looks so fragile. Oh, Dad – do you think …?'

'We must keep on hoping. I'll go and sit with him now.'

'Is this what you're going to do all day – sit by him for a time, and then come here?'

'That's the plan. They suggested ten minutes at a time. I may go out for a bit of a walk, or perhaps have a cup of coffee, but mostly I'll just sit with him, and quietly talk about trains. I believe, in the end, he'll answer.'

Joanna bent down and kissed her father.

'You're such a good man. You don't deserve all the rubbish that's been heaped on you.'

'Oh yes I do,' he replied. 'I've learned quite a lot about myself recently, and I'm not proud of it.'

'I'll come again soon,' she said, 'some time when neither Sarah nor Michael will be here. I promise – and … thanks, Dad.'

Fraser watched her go, and was left with more uncomfortable thoughts to dwell on. Was there to be no end to the shocks he would be subjected to?

Soon Michael arrived. He, too, looked as if he was suffering unbearably. He sank down in a chair, and asked, 'How is he?'

'Still the same,' replied Fraser.

'Oh God!' He put his head in his hands. Then he got up, and without saying anything further went to look at his son.

When he came back Michael looked worse than ever.

'I can't believe this is happening. I can't believe George is lying there in a coma. I've seen him with my own eyes, but I can't seem to grasp it.'

'It's pretty tough to get your head round,' agreed Fraser. 'Only yesterday we were all laughing together, the twins and I. Now everything's different.'

'I feel so bad that you had to take care of them for the day. It wasn't right to put that on you, and it wasn't right that neither Sarah nor I could do it. I wish I had made myself free. The trouble was that I had committed myself to that date some time previously, and it was hard to get out of it.'

'I know, Michael, I know,' said Fraser.

'Yes, of course you do. You were in business. You know how important it is not to let a client down. You soon lose customers if you don't keep your word.'

'I know about it, Michael.'

'Still, I should have tried. I blame myself dreadfully for not trying. I should have been firm and said that I couldn't make it that day.'

'Michael, I know – about you and Joanna.'

Michael had been pale before, but now he turned deathly white.

'You do? How? I mean …'

'Joanna's been here. She told me.'

'She told you!'

'Yes. She's busy hating herself for it as well.'

'I swear to you, Fraser – whatever happens to George – I swear to you that it's finished. I'll never, ever go to her again. I don't know what I was thinking of … I must have been mad. Whatever must you think of me?'

'I understand that Sarah's way of dealing with all her responsibilities is to put a lot of pressure on her family. I know that excuses nothing, but I think she is now aware that perhaps she had lost sight of her priorities. So now it's down to you both – I hope you can find a way of going forward together.'

'What do you mean? I've said it's over with Joanna – of course I'll throw all my energies into helping Sarah now.'

'First,' said Fraser, 'you must tell her.'

It was obvious from Michael's reaction that this had not been on his agenda. He looked shocked, and spluttered, 'No! I couldn't possibly. No, Fraser, I'm sorry – it's just not on.'

'Michael,' replied Fraser firmly, 'if you and Sarah are going to try and pick up the pieces together, then it has to be without guilty secrets. How can you be genuinely close if there is an unspoken deceit between you? You will always be on your guard, in case you let something slip. It has to be a clean slate.'

Michael was silent for a time. Then he said, 'I think it would be a lot better if she didn't know. God knows she has enough to bear at the moment. I really don't think I can add to her burdens. It wouldn't be fair.'

'Have you been fair up to now? Who are you trying to protect – Sarah, or yourself? You must tell her. Of course it will be hard. And of course she'll hate hearing it. But believe me, there's no other way if you really mean to put the past behind you.'

Michael sat there, shaking his head, battling with his feelings. Then, without saying another word, he stood up and walked out.

When he had left Fraser went back to sit with George. He was becoming a familiar figure in the unit now, and the staff smiled at him, encouragingly. For his part he began to understand what went on there each moment of the day and his admiration for those who undertook this critical care nursing grew by the hour. The Staff Nurse in charge was a friendly Asian woman, called Nina Choudhary, who would often come over and have a word with him. Fraser would ask if there was anything more she could tell him, but she would just smile, and say, 'He's still here, Mr Coleman. There's hope as long as he's still here.'

That afternoon Sarah came. Fraser was fairly sure Michael hadn't said anything yet. She was still extremely agitated, but a little calmer – at least she had been able to drive herself down this time. Fraser felt sorry for her – not only for the acute worry she was experiencing – but for what she had still to learn.

His texts to Angela were emotional – he poured out as best he could in such a short message his acute anxiety. There was always a response, in time, and her words brought him some comfort. The most recent said that the trial was almost over, there would be the verdict the next day, and she expected to come back soon. He looked forward to that.

Another day passed, and the only news it brought was from Angela. She reported that the youths had been found guilty – one was sentenced to life imprisonment and the other to twenty years. It was obviously a relief to have a conclusion to the matter. She would try and get a flight back as soon as possible.

On the third day Joanna arrived early, once more. She greeted Fraser and then went straight to George. Then she came back and he realised there was something different about her.

'I've made a decision,' she said. 'I've just been to tell George.' She smiled.'I think he was pleased.'

'What decision?' Fraser waited, aware that this was an important moment for her.

'I know now what I want to do with my life. It's all fallen into place. I want to be a doctor. I want to start my training as soon as possible.'

'A doctor?' Fraser was incredulous.'Are you sure?'

'Absolutely positive – I couldn't be surer of anything. I've enquired about courses, and it seems I may have the necessary A Levels behind me. I believe I can apply for a place this autumn.'

'It's a long, hard training,' said Fraser. 'Do you think you can … ?'

'You mean will I stick at it? I know my record isn't great – but that's because I never found what I really wanted to do. Now I know, and I'm going for it, and I promise I'll see it through. I've promised George I will.'

Fraser began to see her in a different light. He realised he'd been too ready to write her off as the one that didn't achieve, who had no purposeful aim. Now she was presenting herself almost in an authoritarian way, and he liked what he saw.

'I'll support you in any way I can. I think it's a brilliant idea – and do you know what? I think I can see you as a doctor.'

Joanna smiled. 'George thinks it's a good idea too,' she said. 'I'm off to do some research.'

Chapter 27

Fraser was becoming a familiar figure at the hospital. The receptionists always had a cheery greeting for him, and Sister Nina was now a friend. At the hotel Mrs Stanbury never failed to ask solicitously if there was any news, and did everything she could for his comfort. She could always produce a meal for him, no matter what the time was, and nothing was too much trouble. A surprise visitor at the hospital had been the grey-haired lady who had looked after Kate at that fateful time. She had said she hoped he wouldn't think it an intrusion, but she did just want to ask how the little boy was. Then there had been the off-duty lady ambulance driver who had helped at the time of the accident. She had also been to enquire. Fraser was deeply moved by the kindness he met on all sides, coming, as it did from people who had, until so recently, been total strangers.

Two more visitors arrived later that day – Sarah accompanied by Kate. Fraser looked hard at Sarah to try and detect any signs that she knew, but her expression was tightly controlled, giving nothing away. She held Kate's hand and together they came to find Fraser in the waiting room.

Fraser greeted them both and told them there was no further news. Kate looked up at him, her eyes very wide, and her face pale. With a slightly trembling lip she said, 'Grandpa, do you think George will be better soon?'

Fraser struggled to retain his composure. He sat down and drew the little girl towards him.

'We'll all go on hoping. That's what we've got to do. We'll keep sending him our love, and we'll believe he'll soon be back with us.'

Kate obviously wanted to say more. Sarah remained quiet and waited while Kate thought for a bit. Then she spoke and her face crumpled, the tears beginning to roll down her cheeks. 'I wish I hadn't always bossed him about so much. Mummy says I am rather bossy with him. I saw he'd lost his kite, and I saw him begin to run after it, and I shouted to him to stop. I called out and told him to stop! And now I wish I hadn't!' She began to sob, and her small body was racked as she gave way to the emotions which overwhelmed her. Fraser held her closer and tried to comfort her.

'You were trying to help! You were trying to stop him because you knew it was wrong for him to run away! You mustn't blame yourself like this!'

'But …' Kate waited for a break between sobs 'I didn't know … I didn't understand … Mummy's told me, if you tell a man not to do something they do it all the more. I didn't know that. If I hadn't told George to stop, perhaps he wouldn't have kept running off! And anyway, I should have run after him. I'm sure I could have caught up with him if I'd run my very fastest.'

Fraser marvelled at the tortuous thinking a six year old could manage. 'Look Kate, we could all blame ourselves, one way or another, but that doesn't help George. I'm sure Mummy isn't blaming you, is she?'

Kate shook her head. 'No, she isn't. She says if it's anyone's fault, it's hers.'

'Very bad things do happen sometimes, and this time it's happened to our family. We must just all try and help each other. I'm sure you're being a big help to Mummy now.'

Sarah spoke at last. Her voice was very quiet, but firm. 'My little girl is the best little girl a mother could have! She helps me all the time. And I'm very grateful to her because she told me something I didn't know.' Sarah paused for a moment. 'She told me that when George wanted to go to the park after school, and I wouldn't let him because there wasn't time, Kate said George cried himself to sleep that night. I hadn't realised he had minded so much about it. I thought he had accepted that as family we can't always fit in some of the things we might like to do. But if I'd stopped to think about it, I should have realised that sometimes it's more important to make people happy than it is to stick to my own timetable.'

'You always done your best for your family. You've been working so hard for everyone's good.' Fraser couldn't bear to see his daughter suffering any more.

'I thought I was. I really thought I was. But oh, Dad, what a lot I didn't see!'

Fraser began to realise what Sarah was saying. She knew – he felt certain of it.

'I've got so much horribly wrong in my time,' he said. 'Perhaps it's a good thing if you've been forced to have a rethink now. There's lots of time ahead for you all to sort things out.'

Sarah nodded, and led Kate away to see George. Fraser

thought how hard it would be for the little girl to see her brother unconscious and swathed in bandages. He waited anxiously for them to return.

They both seemed much calmer. Kate smiled at Fraser.

'I've told him. I'm sure he heard me. I promised him when he came home I wouldn't keep telling him what to do.' Then she frowned. 'I hope I can remember not to. I might do it before I've stopped to think.' She turned to her mother, looking worried again.

'If I hear you being bossy I'll remind you,' said Sarah. 'And if you hear me not listening to what George is trying to say, you can tell me too.'

They went off together, mother and daughter, closely bound together in their pain. Fraser wondered how it would be when he next saw the parents together.

Chapter 28

The aeroplane hovered at the end of the runway poised, preparing for the moment when it would throw all its energies into the forward thrust that would achieve the marvel of take-off. The crescendo of the mounting engine speed echoed the rising emotions that threatened to burst through Angela's tense body as she attempted, unsuccessfully, to relax in seat 33A. There was only one thing worse than take-off, in her view, and that was coming down to land.

Seat 33B was occupied by a middle-aged man who had not stopped fidgeting since he sat down. He looked in the seat pocket in front of him, took everything out, and then put it all back, one item at a time. Then he started to rummage in his pockets, of which there seemed to be an unlimited number. First his outer coat, then his jacket, then his trouser pockets – and when he had been through all of those he started again on the coat. Then he took the coat off, but was undecided where to stow it. He looked up at the overhead locker as if that might open of its own accord and a hitherto concealed arm reach down and take his coat for him. No such event occurring he put it over one arm and looked from side to side – all seats were occupied – and then behind him. Sighing he rolled the coat up and put it under the seat in front of him. Then he started looking in the seat pocket again! Finally he turned to Angela and remarked that there did not seem to be a sick bag in there.

Great, thought Angela. Here am I, a nervous flier, and I have to find myself sitting next to a man who thinks he might be sick. It was going to be a long flight.

As the ground disappeared from view she tried to interest herself in the magazine provided, and wondered what the inflight entertainment might be. But it was impossible to block out the thoughts which were welling up in her as New York grew more distant, and that phase of her life was now being left behind. She wondered if she would ever go back, and decided she must try and visit Martin's family, especially his ageing parents who had been broken-hearted at the loss of their son. It was no good – she would have to let her thoughts run over the events of the past few weeks, and try to lay them to rest.

The sight of the two youths, lounging back in their seats in the dock, apparently unconcerned at the suffering they had inflicted, and showing no signs of remorse, had been hard to bear. Then there was the young Downs Syndrome woman. She had struggled bravely to give her evidence, and her distress as she was forced to remember the misery of being tormented by the youths had brought tears to the eyes. But worst, of course, had been the reliving of all that happened - the way an evening so full of promise had been wrecked by devastating events – a life full of unselfish service snuffed out in a moment of thoughtless anger.

She had been lucky to have known Martin, and to have had him as her husband. She would never lose sight of that. Surely she, of all people, should be equipped with the knowledge of how to come through this and rise above it. Now there had been closure, with the verdict of guilty and the sentencing of those two youths, it was time to move on. But in what direction?

She thought of Fraser and his family, and of that little boy lying in a coma. Another tragedy that had come out of the blue and threatened to destroy the happiness of all those who were involved. Poor Fraser – he had had so much to bear recently, and had faced up to it all with an impressive courage. She knew he was there at the hospital now, tenderly caring for his grandson, doing everything in his power to will the little boy back to life. Her heart went out to him.

The fidgeting man was still being a trial. When the meal was brought round he could not decide whether to eat it or not, nor which part to attack first. He picked items up and put them down again, sighing in a disconcerting fashion. He struggled to open the packet containing a bread roll and then gave up. The thought of him eating his meal and then not being able to keep it down quite put Angela off hers. She nibbled a small amount and then pushed it away.

She would try and get some sleep, remote though the possibility seemed. The meals were cleared away – with more items seeming to go back into the trolley than had come out in the first place. Angela put her seat back and settled herself down. Her eyes closed, and miraculously her troubled mind began to calm down. She woke to hear the pilot announce that they would shortly be making their descent into Heathrow.

This was the moment she always dreaded. When she flew with Martin she would hold his hand most of the flight, and at this point would squeeze it so hard it was all he could do to repress a cry of pain. She hated the thought of hurtling towards the ground – watching the fields and streets get closer and closer – and couldn't help wondering how on earth this man-made object, bent on its swift downward path, could be restrained sufficiently to allow a gentle landing.

Panic was on the point of setting in when suddenly a warm sensation flooded through her, dispelling the tension. The nearer they got to the ground the more the feeling of joy – perhaps even triumph - took over. She couldn't explain it, but an unmistakable happiness swelled up inside her until she wanted to sing aloud. In place of the usual fear a rising tide of happiness threatened to engulf her. It was as though something wonderful had happened. As the wheels hit the tarmac Angela turned to see her white-knuckled neighbour finally release his grip on the arms of his seat. For the first time on the entire flight he smiled.

'We've landed,' he breathed. 'Thank God.'

'Yes,' replied Angela, beaming at him. 'Thank God.'

Chapter 29

The next day Fraser's question was answered. He was just about to leave the hospital briefly for a breath of fresh air when he saw Michael's car draw up. As soon as it had stopped Michael leaped out and came quickly round to the passenger side where he held the door open for Sarah. Then they walked together towards the hospital entrance holding hands. They were smiling.

Not wanting them to know he had been watching them Fraser quickly retreated to his usual waiting post, where they arrived and greeted him. After the greetings Fraser had to report that there was no change in George's condition. He was still just hanging on.

'Wasn't Kate brave yesterday!' remarked Fraser.'I hope her worries were allayed to some extent, after her visit.'

Sarah's eyes moistened. 'I'm beginning to appreciate what a strong and thoughtful daughter I have. I should have realised it before. She has been a real support to me.'

It was Michael's turn to speak. 'I'm glad she was able to express her feelings to you. We hadn't understood the full extent of the responsibility she had taken on her small shoulders for the accident. You helped her to come to terms with it all and to feel absolved from blame. Thank you for being so caring.'

'That's what grandfathers are for. Perhaps I can still have my uses.' Fraser paused. Then he continued, 'After Edie died I felt useless. I couldn't cook, I couldn't mix with people. I seemed to have lost the whole purpose for living, and my confidence deserted me. Now I've been able, perhaps, in a small way, to become more involved with your family, and to see that I can make my own contribution, I'm feeling better in myself. That sounds strange, when we've all got this dreadful crisis hanging over us.'

'No it doesn't.' Sarah was looking thoughtful. 'I think I understand what you're saying. You see ...' she hesitated. The next bit was going to be difficult. She took a deep breath, and then went on. 'Michael and I have had our own crisis. And I must take much of the blame for that. I was so bent on the day-to-day mechanics of achieving all that had to be done that I lost sight of ...' She was finding the emotion difficult, and had to stop.

Michael took her hand between both of his. 'I'm not going to let Sarah take the responsibility for what I did. I was completely wrong in looking for comfort outside the marriage. I bitterly regret it. Somehow we had lost the ability to talk things over between us. That is never going to happen again. Sarah has been wonderful, and now we are going to see our son, and dedicate our lives together to him, and, of course, to our daughter.'

They went off to the intensive care unit, and when they returned they looked calm – almost happy.

'I don't know how to thank you for keeping up this constant vigil,' said Michael. 'It means a great deal to us to know that you are on the spot, all the time. When something does happen to George – whatever it is – his beloved grandpa will be here with him. That is a great comfort.'

As they left Fraser felt a kind of warm glow. He decided to visit George, and then go out for a brief walk.

The sun shone, and the air was clean and sharp. Sea air had a quality that energised and lifted the spirits. How different from the heavy atmosphere filled with petrol fumes that he normally breathed. He made his way back.

He had scarcely arrived at the waiting room when Sister Nina appeared, agitated. 'Come, quickly, Mr Coleman. Quick! Quick!'

Fraser's heart lurched. 'What is it? Has he …' Fearing the worst, he couldn't bring himself to say the word.

She didn't answer, but urged him towards George's bedside. He looked at the boy, but could see no difference. He must have died peacefully, in his coma. Fraser sank down into the chair and put his head in his hands.

'Look at his eyes! Look at his eyes!' Sister Nina's excitement made Fraser sit up. Were George's eyes open just a fraction? Fraser thought he could see a slit. Then, as he watched, the slit widened. There was unmistakably a gap and some of the eye was showing. Slowly the lids continued their upward movement until a pair of eyes were visible – lifeless, uncomprehending eyes that apparently saw nothing, that expressed nothing.

'Georgie! My dear boy! Hello George – it's Grandpa. Oh George, how wonderful to see you! It's … it's magic!'

And now a light began to creep into those eyes. And the mouth began to move! Was that a smile? It was so hard to tell amongst all those bandages.

Then another miracle happened. George spoke.

'Hello, Grandpa. Grandpa, I really, really hurt.'

'I know, old boy.' Fraser reached under the sheet for George's hand and took hold of it, cradling it between his two large ones. 'The thing is, you've had a nasty accident. In fact, you've been asleep for quite a long time. I've been waiting for you to wake up.'

'Where's Mummy?' The face began to pucker.

'She's been here to see you already today. You were sleeping then, so you didn't know she was there. She came, with Daddy, just a few minutes ago. She's on her way home now, but I'll ring her and tell her you've woken up, and she and Daddy will come straight back. You rest a little more, and they'll soon be here.'

George closed his eyes and Fraser stood up, fishing for his handkerchief. He blew his nose loudly and wiped his eyes, and then turned to see Sister Nina with the tears unashamedly pouring down her cheeks. Fraser clasped her in a great bear hug and swung her round before he put her down.

'I don't know how to thank you – you and all your nursing team. You've all worked so hard to keep him alive, and cared for him – I can't thank you enough!'

'This is our reward. To see a patient recover. It makes it all worth while. I'm so happy for you.'

'I must go and call my daughter.'

Fraser hurried to the hospital exit and switched on his mobile phone. He rang Sarah's number and could hardly speak for the emotion. He heard the heartfelt 'Thank God' they both uttered. They would turn round straight away and be there as soon as possible.

Fraser's phone bleeped telling him a text message had arrived. It was from Angela, and it read, 'Back with you again.'

Fraser smiled. She had an amazing knack for hitting the nail on the head. With a heart lighter than it had been for weeks he went back into the hospital.

Chapter 30

George found that the world to which he returned was rather different from the one he had left, and he rather liked it. Mummy and Daddy were around much more. Mummy now shared the morning school run with Maria, and was always waiting at the school gate when he and Kate were ready to come home at the end of the day. Daddy had time to play games and take them for walks, and sometimes put them to bed. Even Kate was less bossy! The atmosphere had changed, and without George being able to put his small finger on it, he enjoyed the new arrangements.

He was not aware of the details that had brought about this transformation. Sarah had decided to put a full time manager into her business, and only work herself from 10 am to 2.30 pm – and not at all in school holidays. Michael had cut down on the visits which took him far away, and made sure he was back in good time to see the children. If it meant less income, it did. He now knew what was important in his life.

Above all, Sarah and Michael had been able to talk everything through and come to some radical decisions. They had both stood on the brink and stared at the abyss of what could be their failed marriage, and they had both drawn back. Michael was overcome with remorse, unable to understand how he had allowed himself to get caught in such a tangled web of deceit and betrayal. Sarah saw, for the first time, what her unstoppable drive to achieve had cost both her children and Michael. Sarah and Michael stood at George's bedside, that first night he was home, glorying in his return and vowing they would try never to let the children down again. Of course there would be mistakes, but their priorities were now defined.

At school George found he was a hero! The class cheered him when he stomped in, and his classmates all wrote their names on his plaster. Kate found pleasure in being able to give vent to the maternal streak which was never very far from the surface. Both children had learned, in the most painful way, the dangers of today's busy roads.

Fraser returned home, but there were still painful connotations attached to it and he began to feel it would be a good idea to move. The more he thought about it the more he felt it was the right thing to do, and he decided to start on the project without delay. There were, however, still some loose ends to tie up.

The first was his business partner, John. What should he do about him? Before he had come to a conclusion John telephoned and asked if he could come round, as there was something he wanted to discuss.

Sitting opposite, John looked ill at ease, and obviously didn't know where to begin. At last he said, 'I'm thinking of asking you to release me from our partnership. You've helped me to achieve a good living for many years, and I shall always be grateful, but now I feel I need to do something different. Sadie has some idea of moving to Spain, and I think perhaps I should go along with what she wants. She hasn't seemed very well or happy recently.'

'I know, John,' said Fraser.

'It's so important to keep the little woman happy, isn't it?'

'I know, John,' repeated Fraser, 'I know.'

'Things have never felt the same, since Edie died. It's as though a spark has gone out.'

'I know.'

'How you must have suffered, with the shock of it, and everything. I want you to know, I really am most dreadfully sorry.'

'I know, John. I know about everything. I know about you and Edie.'

John froze in his seat and then covered his face with his hands. At last he spoke. 'I thought you must have known before, that Edie must have told you, but when I came to try and apologise I realised you didn't know. I've been in an agony of indecision, but in the end I thought it was kinder to leave you in ignorance. When did you find out? How long have you known?'

'For a few weeks now. It was when I finally plucked up courage to turn out her things. I know about your short breaks and your cruises. You were both very clever, keeping it all secret the way you did. You certainly had me fooled. Well, was she good company? I'm intrigued to know what the financial arrangements were. Did she pay your fare for you? If so, you could say I funded your little jaunts, as that was the money I'd put in a Savings Account for her – to use if anything happened to me. Ironical, isn't it – both of you going off and enjoying yourselves, on my money.'

John hung his head. 'I don't know what to say,' he said.

'Please give me a chance to explain. It was a terrible thing I did, I know – but Edie …'

'I don't want to hear any more,' said Fraser. 'I had thought you a trusted partner and friend. I feel let down by so many people – people I thought well of – people who smiled at me and told me what a good fellow I was. All the time I've been a laughing-stock, a gullible, cuckolded husband. My friends have behaved as enemies, and stabbed me in the back. Go, John. Go off to Spain. Make amends to your Sadie and try and salvage some good years from the mess that has surrounded us all.'

'I don't suppose …' John, hesitated. 'I was wondering if you could find it in your heart to shake my hand? Then I promise you'll never see me again. But I don't think I can go off and start again without some outward sign, at least, of your goodwill, although I know I don't deserve it. I know it's asking an awful lot. I didn't know it was possible to feel so wretched.'

He stood up and proffered his hand. Fraser stood up also and went to the door, which he held open for John. John reached the door, his face contorted with misery. Then Fraser did hold out his hand.

'I wish you both well,' he said. 'I do understand the circumstances – she used you, as she used me, to fulfil her needs – and God, I know how that hurts.'

Briefly the two men gripped hands.

'I'll get a solicitor to draw up the papers terminating our arrangements,' said Fraser.

'Will you carry on with the business?' asked John.

'Possibly, on a much smaller scale. It all depends. I'm making some changes in my life myself. I'll have to see how things work out. Well, that's my affair now. We'll communicate if we need to, but not otherwise.'

The exchange upset Fraser. He hated being confrontational, but he knew he would not have been able to live with himself if he hadn't spoken out. Now there was a ghost he had to lay. He rang Angela.

'How would you like a day trip – to Brighton?'

'That sounds a pleasant idea. I think I can guess the reason.'

'You probably can – well some of the reasons, anyway. I used to love going there – something about the atmosphere – but now the town is full of horrific undertones I can't bear to think about it – it's slid off my map of England. I need to put it back on, by having some pleasant experiences there, in the company of my guardian angel. Please say you'll come.'

The next day – a beautiful sunny one - they had set off. Fraser had planned how he wanted to spend it, and his spirits began to rise as they motored towards the south coast. Angela was aware that the day was important to him, and that he had wounds to heal. She chatted lightly, and asked him where he planned to go first.

'I thought, if you were happy with the idea, we'd go to the Pavilion.'

They both enjoyed wandering round this eccentric, Indian style piece of English culture with its opulent rooms, but the dazzling Music Room with its domed ceiling of gilded scallop-shaped shells took their breath away.

'Magic!' breathed Fraser.

Angela laughed. 'Follow that! Where shall we go now?'

They went to The Lanes, and Angela was in her element poking about in the shops. A necklace with an amethyst pendant caught her attention and she enthused about it to Fraser.

'I'm getting hungry,' he said. 'Would you have a look at the menu in that bistro over there and see if it appeals to you? I'll look just look at this one.'

She obediently crossed the lane as she was asked, and in a few moments Fraser joined her. He was holding a small box.

'I'd like you to accept this. It's a small token of thanks for all you've done for me and my family over the past weeks. I really don't know how I'd have managed without you.'

Angela opened the box and the cut glass amethyst twinkled at her.

'Oh Fraser! How lovely! You really shouldn't have – but I'll accept it in the spirit in which it was given. Thank you very much!' She planted a kiss on his cheek. Fraser was a little embarrassed.

'Come on,' he said. 'Let's go in. As George would say – I'm starving!'

They sat down and studied the menu.

'Fish and chips or sausages and baked beans?' asked Fraser.

'Is one or the other obligatory?'

'It is if you're young.'

'There are, it seems, some distinct advantages to being old. I'll settle for the salmon.'

Fraser decided to order the roast lamb, and they passed a happy, relaxed hour enjoying a good meal in pleasant surroundings.

'I hope you don't mind my asking,' said Fraser, over the coffee, 'but I've been thinking about all you've been through. And I was wondering if you now feel you have been able to draw a line under the past?'

'Of course I don't mind. The court case was very

difficult at the time, as you know, but it has helped. At least I can feel that justice was done. Nothing can ever right the wrong, nor bring Martin back, but I think I've been able to reach the point where I can be glad for the years we had, and start to look forward.'

'What do you look towards?' asked Fraser. 'Or is that rather too personal a question?'

'You can ask, but at the moment my ideas are not sufficiently well finalised to give you a specific answer. I'm still thinking.'

Fraser nodded. 'Let's go and look at the sea,' he said.

'Do you want to go on the pier?'

'I think I must, but first I'd like to just go down to the promenade. Then I'll buy you a stick of rock and you can buy me a kiss-me-quick hat.'

'Wouldn't suit you,' she replied. 'And a stick of rock would break my teeth.'

They walked down to the pier and then sat on a bench looking out to sea. Fraser found his attention absorbed by the waves breaking continuously on the pebbles. How many people must have watched them doing that, over the years, and would no doubt go on doing so in the future.

'I keep thinking about my father,' he said. 'I believe he loved my mother very much, and his children, too. It must have been dreadful for him to leave home and go to Poland, knowing that he could well not be coming back.'

'It was a very sacrificial thing he did.'

After a pause Fraser said, 'It's strange to think that Edie's father was in the war too, but on the other side. I wonder if the two fathers ever came up against each other in the conflict? I imagine that's a very remote possibility.'

'Yes, very remote.'

'After all, Edie's father would have had to have been in Warsaw as well.'

'That's true,' agreed Angela.

'Well, I suppose that's something we'll never know.'

'No,' agreed Angela. 'You'll never know.'

'Right,' said Fraser. 'Now the pier, and then we have to walk down to the sea.'

'Oh dear – my shoes aren't very suitable for the pebbles.'

'I know what – we can go on the pier and I'll buy you some jellies. Or would you prefer crocs? Everyone wears them.'

'One lovely present is enough for today. Don't worry – I'm sure I'll manage.'

They walked through the turnstile, Fraser retracing his steps, hearing the twins' laughter in his ears and their excited cries. Suddenly he found he was concentrating on the happiness they had all enjoyed rather than dwelling on the tragic part.

'Let's go down to the beach now!' Clasping Angela's hand he began to pull her towards the promenade, and down the steps. Sure enough she was soon losing her footing and started stumbling on the pebbles. Fraser caught hold of her arm and together they slipped and slid their way down to the water's edge.

'Throwing stones into the sea is obligatory,' said Fraser. 'I see with relief there's some left. Kate worried George was going to throw them all into the sea.'

Angela chose a couple of flat ones and launched the pebbles seawards, but they failed to bounce, sinking like the proverbial stone.

'I see your education has been sadly lacking in the pebble-skimming department,' remarked Fraser.

'I think I was off sick that week. You'd better show me how it's done.'

Fraser bent to select some, and then tossed them over the water, achieving three highly satisfactory bounces before they disappeared from sight.

'Very good,' commented Angela. 'You are indeed an accomplished man.'

Fraser was silent for a moment. Then he said, conversationally, 'I suppose you wouldn't consider marrying me?'

'Why would I want to do that?' she asked.

'Well, for starters, there's my handsome looks and immense wealth.'

'Irresistible attractions indeed,' she replied. 'But I was rather hoping for something more.'

'Well,' he said, and stopped.

'Yes?' prompted Angela.

'The thing is ...'

She waited.

'The thing is,' resumed Fraser, 'I do a very nice line in kitchens. What do you say?'

Now it was Fraser's turn to have to wait.

'I think ...' began Angela.

'Yes?' he asked anxiously.

'I think that would be magic,' she said.

Laughing, and with their arms round each other's waists, they clambered back over the pebbles and made for home.

About the Author

Monica Carly graduated from Bristol University with an Honours Degree in English, French and Latin and a teaching qualification. Whilst raising a family she took a creative writing course and produced several short stories. She has taught English in schools and as a foreign language, studied Graphology and taught this in evening classes, qualified in consumer law, and recently in proofreading. 'Fraser's Line' is her first full length novel.

Printed in the United Kingdom by
Lightning Source UK Ltd., Milton Keynes
139714UK00001B/3/P